Vatsana's
Lucky New Year

Sara Gogol

Lerner Publications Company
Minneapolis, Minnesota

Library of Congress Cataloging-in-Publication Data

Gogol, Sara
 Vatsana's lucky new year / Sara Gogol.
   p.   cm.
 Summary: Torn between Laotian and American cultures, twelve-year-old
Vatsana faces prejudice from a boy at school as she helps her newly arrived
Laotian cousin adjust to life in Portland, Oregon.
 ISBN 0-8225-0734-X
 [1. Laotian Americans—Fiction. 2. Prejudices—Fiction. 3. Schools—
Fiction. 4. Cousins—Fiction]. I. Title.
PZ7.G5584Vat   1992
[Fic]—dc20

                                                                11243
                                                                 CIP
                                                                  AC

Manufactured in the United States of America

1 2 3 4 5 6 97 96 95 94 93 92

Acknowledgments

I could not have written this book without the generous help of several people in the Portland Lao community. Tou Meksavanh, Lavanny Phommaneth, Tara Phommaneth, and Pat Chanthabouasy patiently answered my many questions about Lao culture and the refugee experience. Additionally, the Southeast Asian students I have taught, who shared their experiences with me, helped give me the idea for Vatsana's story.

I would like to thank Julie Allen, Diane Averill, Molly Gloss, Reva Leeman, and Winnie Schechter for reading the manuscript of *Vatsana's Lucky New Year* at various stages of its development and for the helpful suggestions they made. Elaine Carter read drafts of the manuscript and her friendship helped encourage me to keep on writing.

Finally, my parents—Rose Edelstein Gogol and Sam Gogol—indirectly inspired this book. As the children of immigrants from Eastern Europe, they each lived through their own versions of Vatsana's experience.

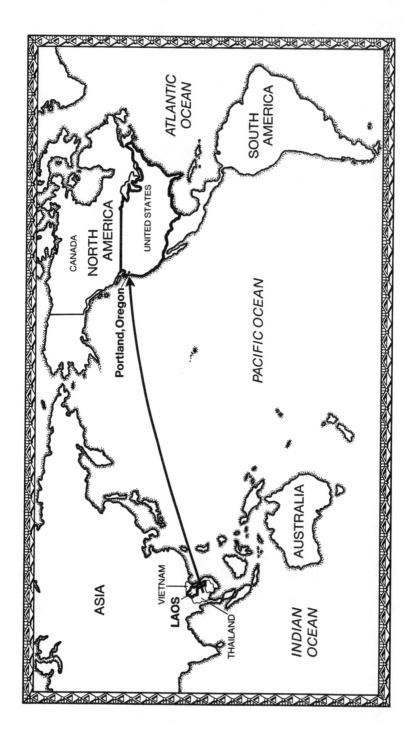

1

Vatsana kicked a piece of ice along the street. Kicking the ice made her think about Tom Connors, the creepy boy in her class at school. She'd never been mean to him, but he was always saying dumb things to her—like calling her "teacher's pet"—or staring at her with an angry look on his face.

Vatsana kicked the ice again and watched it skitter along the sidewalk. She wished she could kick out at Tom Connors like that, easily and lightly, and make him stop bothering her.

The strong east wind pushed at her back. She forgot about the piece of ice and walked faster now. It only got cold enough to have snow and ice in Portland every year or two.

"Too cold," her mother always said then. That was because her mother was from Laos, a much warmer country in Southeast Asia. But Vatsana had been born right here in Portland, Oregon. And she liked the cold weather.

She slid a little as she turned the corner to her house. The sidewalk was still icy in spots, but her older brother Vyvone had cleared all the snow and ice off the steps leading to the house. Her house was raised up above the street, like most of the houses in her neighborhood.

The front porch had an overhanging roof which kept things dry in the rainy season. She stopped on the porch to pick up the mail. Then she let herself into the house.

She quickly leafed through the batch of mail, just in case there was something for her. She didn't find anything with her own name on it, but there was a letter for her mother and father. One of the stamps had a picture of an elephant on it, so Vatsana knew the letter was from Thailand, the country across the Mekong River from Laos.

The letter helped her to stop thinking about Tom Connors. She felt herself letting go of the worried feeling in her stomach that Tom Connors gave her. The letter must be from her aunt Lavanny. Aunt Lavanny and her daughter Ketsy were staying in a refugee camp in Thailand right now. As soon as they could get permission, they were going to come to the United States. After they arrived, they would live with Vatsana's family.

Vatsana took off her winter jacket and hung it up in the hall closet. Since she'd worn jeans to school that day, she didn't need to change. Instead she went into the kitchen to get something to eat. She took out a bag of cookies from the cupboard and poured herself a glass of milk.

She bit into a cookie, letting the chocolate chip part melt in her mouth. Her cousin Ketsy was the same age as she. So she guessed Ketsy would like chocolate chip cookies too. Vatsana reached for another cookie. It was hard to think about a cousin she'd never met. Vatsana's mother and father and older brother had escaped from Laos before either Vatsana or Ketsy were born.

Vatsana was just finishing her milk when she heard the front door open. Her mother must be home from work. She worked at the Wexco Company, which made different kinds of electronic equipment.

Vatsana rinsed out her glass and put the cookies away. Then she went into the living room. Her mother was sitting in the armchair near their shrine to Buddha, reading the letter. She had an excited look on her face. When she finished it, she gave Vatsana a big smile.

"Your aunt Lavanny says that she and Ketsy will come to Portland soon," her mother said in Lao. "After so long our family will be together."

"That's good," Vatsana said. It did sound nice even though she wasn't super excited herself. Aunt Lavanny was her mother's sister, and Vatsana knew that having Aunt Lavanny and Ketsy come here meant a lot to her mother.

"*Saa tu*," Vatsana's mother said, which was the Lao way of saying how thankful she was. "For so many years we've written letters. And now we'll see each other again." She looked at Vatsana. "You'll finally meet your aunt Lavanny and your cousin Ketsy."

When Vatsana's mother went into the kitchen to start fixing dinner, Vatsana followed her. She figured her mother was in the mood to talk, and since Aunt Lavanny and Ketsy were coming, Vatsana wanted to hear more about them.

"Your aunt Lavanny and I are only two years apart," her mother said while she pulled out vegetables and cooking pots. When we were growing up we were always close friends. We did everything together."

Her mother pounded some spices with a mortar and pestle. Then she added them to the salad and mixed everything together. She smiled at Vatsana. "Now you and Ketsy can be good friends too. Ketsy is a nice girl. She does well in school just like you. I know the two of you are going to like each other. Soon you'll be just like sisters."

Vatsana hoped that her mother was right. She'd always wanted a sister. And it was neat that Ketsy was 12 years old, the same age she was.

Just then Vatsana's older brother, Vyvone, and her younger brother, Souk, came in. "Hi little sister," Vyvone said to Vatsana. Vyvone was 19, with a slim but strong build like their father and straight black hair like they all had. Vyvone was in his first year at the community college, so he tried to act as if he were all grown up.

Souk grinned at Vatsana. He was eight years old, stockier than Vyvone, and really cute with his big brown eyes and quick smile. He was definitely her favorite brother.

Souk started telling everybody all the things that had happened at his Cub Scout meeting. And of course Vatsana's mother told both Souk and Vyvone about the letter from Aunt Lavanny. As usual, their father came home from work just before dinner. He worked for an agency that helped refugees, and his job kept him busy.

Vatsana's father was taller than most Lao men, which Vatsana was glad about. "*Sa bai dee*," he said. That meant "hello" in Lao. He gave his usual gentle smile. He smiled even more when Vatsana's mother gave him the letter.

While Vatsana's father read the letter from Aunt Lavanny, Vatsana laid the woven straw mat down on the living room floor and helped her mother put the dishes of food into the round bamboo serving tray. Then her mother carried in the tray.

They all sat on the mat around the bamboo tray and helped themselves to baked fish, sticky rice, vegetables, and salad. That was the Lao way to eat together, and it was one of the customs Vatsana's mother and father wanted to keep.

Vatsana's father stopped eating for a moment. Sometimes he told stories and jokes at dinner, but tonight he had a serious look on his face. "We're very lucky that your aunt Lavanny and cousin Ketsy can come to the United States. Some families have to stay for many years in refugee camps. But because your mother and I are American citizens now, we can sponsor Aunt Lavanny and Ketsy, so they don't have to wait so long."

"When are they coming?" Vatsana asked.

Her father frowned at her because she'd spoken English. "Did you forget how to speak Lao?" he asked her. Her father spoke good English and her mother's English was pretty good. But at home they almost always spoke Lao.

Vatsana shook her head. She looked down at the table. Sometimes she remembered to speak Lao, but other times she just naturally started talking in English. She'd spoken English all her life after all, and it was easier for her to speak English than Lao.

"We don't live in Laos," she'd said to her father once. "We live in America. So why do I have to speak Lao so much or go to the special classes to learn to read and write Lao?"

Her father had been angry with her then, even though he hardly ever got angry with her or Souk or Vyvone. "Laos is still our home country," he had said in a stern voice. "You are all Lao children too. You need to learn about your family's home country. That's why you need to know Lao."

Vatsana hadn't said anything else to her father then. "America is my country," she imagined herself saying to him now. She wished that her father and mother would understand that more.

Her father and mother were still talking about Aunt Lavanny and her daughter Ketsy. "When are they going to be here?" Vatsana asked again, in Lao this time.

Her mother gave Vatsana the approving smile that meant she thought Vatsana was being a good daughter. "We're not sure when they'll be here," her father said. "Probably in a few weeks. Maybe sooner."

"Ketsy can share your room with you," her mother said.

11

Vatsana didn't say anything. She hadn't thought about where Aunt Lavanny and Ketsy would stay. But it figured that Ketsy would share her room. Vyvone and Souk were already sharing a room.

When Vatsana was finished eating she pressed her palms together, made a little bow, and said, *"Saa tu."* Her mother and father liked her to do that because it was the Lao custom. It meant that she was thankful for the food.

Her parents were still talking when Vatsana went upstairs to her room. She shut the door, sat down on her chair, and looked around the room. Over her bed was the picture of Mount Hood she'd put up. And on the other wall, over her bureau, there was the picture of two bear cubs playing, which she'd gotten at the Washington Park Zoo last year. She liked looking at that picture because the cubs were so cute.

The pictures were hers and the room was all hers. Or it had been ever since her parents had bought this house a few years ago. She could read here or do her homework or just be alone and think her own thoughts. Sometimes she sat at her desk and wrote down stories she made up. Little by little, she was filling up the book with blank pages and a red cloth cover which Vyvone had given her for her last birthday.

What would it feel like to share her room with Ketsy? In the photograph Aunt Lavanny had sent, Ketsy was smiling at the camera. She had long hair tied back behind her face and she was wearing the Lao long skirt and a long-sleeved yellow blouse. She looked very foreign, Vatsana thought.

Ketsy had grown up in Laos instead of the United States as Vatsana had. So she wouldn't know any English. Or maybe just a little, if she had learned some in the refugee camp. Probably Vatsana would have to bring Ketsy along when she spent time with her best friend, Becky Kamminsky. Becky and her mother had moved into a house on Vatsana's block at the beginning of the summer, and ever since, she and Vatsana had been friends.

It would be boring for Becky to sit and listen to Vatsana and Ketsy talking in Lao. Besides, Vatsana liked spending time alone with Becky. They could talk about all kinds of things and make up crazy games. She didn't know if it would feel the same with Ketsy there too.

Vatsana sat down at her desk and took out her math book. She wasn't at all sure that Ketsy would really be like a sister. But she and Becky could teach Ketsy about the United States. Then maybe the three of them could be friends.

Mrs. O'Malia had auburn hair which curled around her head, clear blue eyes, and a quick smile. She was Vatsana's favorite teacher because she was so nice and because Vatsana liked English and social studies. In Mrs. O'Malia's class, they studied both of these.

"Are you ready to start the Middle Ages tomorrow?" Mrs. O'Malia asked them.

Some of the kids groaned. "I don't even shave yet," one of the boys said, making his voice high and funny sounding.

Everybody laughed at that, including Mrs. O'Malia. "Well, maybe you'll all have aged enough by tomorrow," she said. Mrs. O'Malia liked a good joke, Vatsana thought. But she never let the kids get too wild or nasty with their jokes, the way her math teacher, Mr. Hansen, did.

The bell rang a minute later. Vatsana waited for her friend Becky outside the room and they walked to the cafeteria and waited in line together the way they usually did.

The lunch choices for today were macaroni-and-cheese and sloppy joes on a bun. Becky got the sloppy joe, and Vatsana got macaroni-and-cheese. That was one of Vatsana's favorite American foods and she was always trying to persuade her mother to make it.

Vatsana and Becky sat down at one end of a long table. "My aunt Lavanny and cousin Ketsy are coming to Portland soon," Vatsana said. "They're still in a refugee camp in Thailand right now, but my mother and father are going to be their sponsors so they can come over here."

"Hey," Becky said, "that's great. When are they coming?"

"Pretty soon," Vatsana said.

"I want to meet your cousin when she comes. And I bet my mom will want to meet your aunt. I know she really likes your mom."

Becky's mom worked as a social worker at Providence Hospital. She was as friendly as Becky was, and Vatsana liked her. Vatsana's mother thought it was too bad that Becky's mom and dad had gotten divorced about a year ago. Divorce wasn't the custom in Laos. But Vatsana was glad that Becky and her mom had moved into Vatsana's neighborhood.

"They won't know English at first," Vatsana said. She pictured her mother introducing Aunt Lavanny and Ketsy to everyone anyway. Her mother never felt shy or afraid of what other people would think the way Vatsana often did.

Vatsana and Becky zigzagged past other kids as they walked down the hallway toward the locker they shared. Then Becky got out her health book and Vatsana took out her math book and notebook. After lunch, Vatsana had math with Mr. Hansen.

Vatsana always did okay in math, but thinking about Mr. Hansen's class gave her a lump-in-the-stomach kind of feeling, partly because of Mr. Hansen, but mostly because of Tom Connors. She wished that Becky were in the class with her. That would make the class feel a little better anyway.

She walked slowly toward Mr. Hansen's class. The bell rang just as she got there. Mr. Hansen was standing in the front of the classroom and he frowned at her as she walked to her seat. Mr. Hansen liked to start class right away. Vatsana sat toward the back of the room, right in front of Tom Connors, because Mr. Hansen made them sit alphabetically and

Chanthavone, Vatsana's last name, came before Connors.

Tom Connors was tall for his age, but he slouched behind his desk. He had red hair and lots of freckles on his face. As usual, he scowled at her as she slid into her seat.

She watched Mr. Hansen mark off the names in his roll book. Mr. Hansen had thinning blonde hair, cold blue eyes, and light-colored eyebrows which always seemed to be fading into his face. He hardly ever smiled, except once in a while when he tried to make a joke. But mostly the kids didn't laugh at Mr. Hansen's jokes.

Vatsana had heard one boy say that this was Mr. Hansen's first year of teaching. A lot of the time, he had a nervous look on his face. Maybe that was why the kids didn't listen to him very well. Mr. Hansen was pretty good at explaining new stuff in math. But he wasn't much good at all at stopping the kids from joking around in class. And he never seemed to notice when Tom Connors bothered her.

Mr. Hansen finished taking roll and stood in front of the class, waiting for them to quiet down. It took a while, but finally most of the kids grew quieter. "All right class," Mr. Hansen said. "Open your books to page 86."

Some of the kids took their time about getting out their books and opening them to the right page. Tom Connors dropped his book on the floor—on purpose, Vatsana figured. He slowly picked up his book and finally opened it to the right page.

Mr. Hansen had given them some of the problems on page 86 to do for homework. "Do you have any questions about the homework problems?" he asked them now.

When nobody said anything, Mr. Hansen cleared his throat. "If you didn't have any questions, let's see how you did on them."

Mr. Hansen called on Dick Adams, a short, fat boy with curly brown hair. He did the problem part-way and then couldn't finish it. Some of the kids laughed and cheered, and one boy pounded on his desk.

"That's enough of that," Mr. Hansen said. But his voice didn't sound strong enough. The kids kept on laughing and joking around while Mr. Hansen finished the problem himself.

Mr. Hansen looked around the room. Vatsana tried not to meet his eyes, but he ended up looking at her anyway. "How about you, Vatsana?" he said, "Do you think you can do the next problem?"

Vatsana felt her hands start to sweat. The lump-in-her-stomach feeling grew stronger. She nodded unhappily. "Teacher's pet," she heard Tom Connors hiss at her as she stood up and walked toward the board.

The problem wasn't too difficult and Vatsana worked it quickly. "That was well done, Vatsana," Mr. Hansen said. Vatsana tried not to look at anybody as she walked back to her seat, but she couldn't help hearing some of the kids laughing.

As she was sitting down again, Tom Connors poked her in the back. "That was easy for you, huh?" he whispered. "I bet you think you're the smartest one in the whole class."

Vatsana didn't say anything back to Tom. She made herself stare at the page of math problems in front of her. That was the best thing to do when Tom Connors gave her a hard time. That way he usually stopped bothering her pretty soon.

A few minutes later the bell rang. Vatsana stood up quickly, grabbed her books, and left the room. She was always glad to get out of Mr. Hansen's class.

She had one more class after math class. That was her science class with Mr. Goldberg. Mr. Goldberg had gray hair, a short moustache, and laugh lines around his eyes. He smiled a lot and made jokes that were a lot funnier than Mr. Hansen's. After Mrs. O'Malia, Mr. Goldberg was Vatsana's favorite teacher. Vatsana liked studying science too. It was interesting to learn about things like atoms, which you would never know about otherwise.

Usually Vatsana enjoyed listening to Mr. Goldberg talk. He had a nice, deep-sounding voice. But today she only halfway paid attention. She was still thinking about Tom Connors and the way he'd called her "teacher's pet" in Mr. Hansen's class.

It wasn't the first time Tom had said something creepy like that. She hadn't ever done anything bad to him, but he always acted as if he didn't like her. Not that she cared what he thought of her. She just wanted him to leave her alone. But he kept on bothering her.

One time when her brother Vyvone wasn't too busy with his schoolwork, she had asked him what he thought about Tom Connors. "Just ignore him," was what Vyvone had said. "Don't let him know that he bothers you, or he'll just pick on you more."

Vyvone was probably right, Vatsana thought. Anyway, she couldn't exactly start arguing with Tom Connors right in the middle of Mr. Hansen's class. Her mother and father always talked about how students in Laos respected their teachers and never talked in class except when they were called on. Her parents knew that American schools were different, but if they ever found out she'd been causing trouble in class, she didn't think they'd care about what Tom Connors had said. They'd just be really mad at her.

Mr. Goldberg finished explaining about how the weather patterns worked in Oregon. Then he asked the class if anyone had seen what the climate was like in different places.

A girl who sat in the front row raised her hand and told about the weather in Colorado. Dan Nguyen, a boy who was from a Vietnamese family, talked about what the weather was like in Vietnam.

Vatsana could have told the class about the monsoon rains in Laos, because her mother had told her stories about what the monsoon season was like. But she figured weather in Laos was probably a lot like Vietnamese weather. And anyway, she didn't think most of the kids were interested in hearing about places like Vietnam and Laos.

"Don't forget that your science projects are due next week," Mr. Goldberg reminded them. Then the bell rang and school was done for the day.

Vatsana picked up her books and headed for her locker. She liked school pretty well—except for Mr. Hansen's class and that jerky Tom Connors. But it was always nice when school was over and she and Becky could walk home together.

A week later Vatsana's mother and father got a phone call from the refugee agency in Portland. The woman from the agency told them that Aunt Lavanny and Ketsy would be coming to Portland next Sunday.

Aunt Lavanny and Ketsy would be here really soon, Vatsana thought. That was exciting, but a little bit scary too.

Vatsana's mother was too busy to tell Vatsana any more about Aunt Lavanny and Ketsy. She went shopping for some of the special foods, like coconut and lemon grass, she would need to cook for Aunt Lavanny and Ketsy. Then she washed the sheets and blankets for the couch in the family room. The couch

22

folded out into a bed, and Aunt Lavanny was going to sleep there.

Vatsana's father found a single bed for Ketsy that would fit next to Vatsana's bed. Vatsana watched as Vyvone and her father carried it up the stairs and set it up in her room.

"You're lucky. Now you have two beds," Vatsana'a father said jokingly.

Vatsana didn't laugh. She still wasn't that happy about having to share her room. It looked too crowded now, not nearly as nice as it had before.

On Saturday, Vatsana's mother told her that she wanted her to help clean the house. Sometimes Vatsana argued with her mother, even though her mother told her that in Laos children always obeyed their parents. But today Vatsana could tell that her mother wouldn't change her mind.

"What about Souk and Vyvone?" she did ask her mother.

"Vyvone will help his father today. Then he needs to study for his college classes. And Souk will help a little, but you know he's too young to do much," her mother answered.

In Laos, Vatsana's mother had told her, girls helped with the cooking, cleaning, and shopping, and boys did things like working in the yard. Vatsana was glad that her mother had more modern ideas—maybe because she'd been to college in Laos and in the United States. She usually made Souk and Vyvone help in the house too.

Vatsana helped her mother clean house all morning. They swept and mopped all the floors, vacuumed the rugs, dusted the family pictures on the wall of the living room and everything else that could hold any dust, and changed the sheets on all the beds. Souk helped too for a while and then he went over to a friend's house to play.

Vatsana's family had been living in this house for a few years, and she pretty much liked the way it looked. Maybe she would change some things. Like the picture of the Buddhist temple and the picture of Buddha on the wall. They looked too foreign, Vatsana thought sometimes. Mostly though she really liked her house. And she liked being here today with just her mother.

By lunch time, the house was looking spotless. Vatsana's mother smiled at Vatsana. "You're a good daughter," she said in English. Hearing her mother say that gave Vatsana a warm feeling inside. Vatsana's mother switched to speaking in Lao. "We work hard today. Now we'll cook and eat just you and me." Vatsana followed her into the kitchen. Even though she wished her mother would cook more American food, she still liked watching her make Lao foods. Her mother was a fine cook, their father always said.

Her mother had been a nurse when they lived in Laos. Her hands were strong and skillful, as a nurse's hands would have to be. Sometimes Vatsana would look at her own hands and wonder if they would look the same as her mother's some day.

Her mother chopped up cooked chicken, raw cabbage, mint leaves, cilantro, and some bean sprouts. She made some rice noodles and then she cooked everything together with some chicken soup. That made a Lao noodle soup, which both Vatsana and her mother liked.

"You're still a growing girl," her mother said to Vatsana. She was smiling and laughing a little at the same time. "After you work hard, you need to eat."

Her mother sat down at the table too. "Maybe I'm growing too," she said. "I think I'm going to eat also." Then her mother switched from Lao to English. "Eat like a pig, yes?"

Vatsana laughed. Her mother could be really fun to be with sometimes.

Her mother went back to talking in Lao. "Your aunt Lavanny and your cousin Ketsy will be here tomorrow." Her voice sounded happy when she said that.

Vatsana ate some of the noodle soup. "What time is their plane coming in?"

25

Vatsana's mother looked a little bit worried. "At twelve o'clock. But we have to be at the airport earlier just in case their plane is early. It would be terrible if we weren't there to meet Aunt Lavanny and Ketsy."

Vatsana's mother ate some more of her soup. She smiled across the table at Vatsana. "When I think about your aunt Lavanny coming tomorrow all my memories come back to me. I remember how much fun we had together when we were younger."

"On many weekends and on school vacations we would take a bus to Ban Keun, the village where our family was from before they moved to Vientiane. Our grandma still lived in Ben Keun and we would stay with her."

Vatsana's mother had talked about the village before, but Vatsana still liked to hear about it. It was funny to think of her mother being the same age as Vatsana was now. "What did you do in Ban Keun?" she prompted her mother.

"In the hot weather we swam in the Nam Ngum," her mother continued. "*Nam*" was the Lao word for river. "But we didn't wear swimsuits. We took our long skirts and wore them high up so they covered our chests and part of our legs." Vatsana's mother laughed. "Sometimes the boys would dive under the water and try to pull our skirts down. So we had to pull up pieces of the river grass and throw it at them."

"That sounds like fun," Vatsana said. She tried to picture her mother swimming in the river in a long skirt.

"We did have a lot of fun in Ban Keun," her mother said. "We would go out to the fields and pick fruit—mangoes and papaya, tamarind and coconut. Then early in the morning we would go to the market. All the people would come from the countryside into the market and they all would bring things to sell—chickens, fruit, vegetables, and things they made, like baskets for sticky rice."

Vatsana's mother smiled. "That market started early—six o'clock in the morning. So Lavanny and I would have breakfast there—big bowls of Lao noodle soup. We would eat our soup and then go look at everything in the market. We liked to look before we decided what to buy."

"I guess that was different from shopping at Safeway, huh?" Vatsana said.

Vatsana's mother laughed. "Very different." She looked at Vatsana more seriously then. "Maybe someday you can go see the market."

"Maybe," Vatsana said. She couldn't make herself sound that enthusiastic. She liked hearing about when her mother was a girl, but she wasn't all that excited about seeing the village for herself.

Vatsana's mother sighed. "It's all just a story to you, isn't it?" She took a drink of her tea. "It's hard for children to understand what's important. My father knew. He wanted to teach his children to play the *khene*, so we would always have Lao music as part of our lives."

The *khene*, Vatsana knew, was a Lao wind instrument made of two rows of bamboo pipes. She'd seen people playing the *khene* at Lao holidays but it was hard to imagine her mother playing it.

Vatsana's mother finished her cup of tea. "I tried to learn the *khene* for a while, because I couldn't disobey my father. But I was busy with other things. And I didn't really see why playing the *khene* was so important. So after a while I just gave it up."

Her mother cleared their plates and started washing the dishes. Vatsana still sat at the table. She was trying to follow a thought in the back of her mind, but it wasn't coming clear yet.

Her mother had obeyed her father, Vatsana's grandfather, and tried to learn to play the *khene*. But she hadn't really wanted to do that.

I go to classes to learn to read and write Lao, Vatsana thought, because my father and mother tell me to. But I don't really want to either. So I don't work anywhere near as hard at it as I do with my regular schoolwork.

"You and me...we're kind of the same you know," Vatsana said all of a sudden to her mother. She still wasn't exactly sure what she wanted to say.

Vatsana's mother smiled. "If you want to see what the elephant will be like, look at its tail." That was a Lao expression which meant that children would be like their parents.

"You didn't work hard at learning to play the *khene*, even though your father told you to," Vatsana said, "because there were other things you wanted to do. That's the same with me. I don't really want to go to the Lao school and learn to read and write Lao. So I don't work hard at that either."

Vatsana's mother was listening but not saying anything.

"I don't need to read and write Lao," Vatsana continued. "I go to an American school and that's what's important for me."

Vatsana didn't say anymore. She didn't want to make her mother mad. Vatsana's mother didn't seem angry though. Instead her face looked sad.

"I gave up practicing the *khene* after a while," her mother said, "and I never really learned how to play it well. But now I'm sorry about that."

She looked at Vatsana. "Your life is so different in America. Sometimes it's hard for your father and me to understand that all the way." She spoke slowly now. "But we do understand one thing. We have to teach you Lao language and customs. If we don't do that, someday you'll be grown up and you'll look at yourself and see that part of you is missing. Maybe only a small part of you, but an important one. And by then it will be too late for you to get it back."

Vatsana's mother didn't say anything more. She sat facing Vatsana, just looking at her for a moment. Her expression was serious but still not angry, Vatsana saw.

Vatsana's mother left the kitchen then. A minute later, Vatsana went upstairs to her room. She sat at her desk and looked out her window at the cloudy sky and the bare branches of trees. A steady rain was just starting to come down.

She got out the book she was reading for fun—a fantasy about a girl on another planet—and tried to concentrate on that but after a few minutes she decided that she couldn't.

She laid down the book and stared out the window again. Part of her might be missing someday, her mother had said, and then it would be too late to get it back. Her mother had been so serious and sad at the same time when she said that.

Vatsana imagined a part of herself running away from the rest of herself. Running down the street and disappearing. That made her think of pictures of missing children. Each picture, someone gone who might never return.

Vatsana poked herself in the arm. Her arm was skinny as always, but it felt solid. Except for being too shy, she felt solid inside herself too. At least most of the time.

So what if she didn't want to learn about Lao stuff? She didn't see how that would make a missing part of her.

Anyway, it was probably a waste of time to talk to her mother about things like the Lao language classes. Usually she and her mother could talk okay. But sometimes—especially when her mother had Lao ideas in her head and Vatsana had American ideas—she felt like that girl she was reading about from another planet.

4

Sunday morning Vatsana woke up as it was beginning to get light. Today was the day. Her aunt Lavanny and cousin Ketsy were coming to Portland today. She'd never met either of them before, but tonight Ketsy would be sleeping in this room with her.

Vatsana threw back the covers and got out of bed. She went to the bathroom and took a shower. Afterward she stared at her face in the bathroom mirror. Her eyes and nose and skin looked Asian even though she felt American inside. Maybe Aunt Lavanny and Ketsy would think Vatsana was really a Lao girl.

Vatsana made a face at the girl in the mirror. She hung up her towel and went back to her room. Her stomach felt a little nervous. She carefully chose a pair of dark blue slacks, a light blue turtleneck, and her new green sweater, instead of the jeans and sweatshirt she mostly wore on weekends.

She went downstairs and into the kitchen. Souk was up already too. He was sitting at the table eating a bowl of cereal and talking to their mother while she did some last minute cooking and cleaning. *"Sa bai dee,"* her mother said to Vatsana. Then she kept on working.

Vatsana poured cereal into a bowl, added some milk to it, and sat down at the table across from Souk. "We're going to the airport in a little while," Souk said excitedly. He grinned at her.

As if she didn't know, Vatsana thought. Souk's excitement was catching though, and she grinned back at him. She wasn't entirely glad Aunt Lavanny and Ketsy were coming, but she was excited too. She was curious about what Ketsy and her aunt Lavanny would be like.

"I just wish Aunt Lavanny had a boy my age," Souk said to Vatsana.

That was about the hundredth time Souk had said that. She couldn't resist teasing him. "Don't worry," she told him. "You and Ketsy and I can all play together. We'll be the doctor and the nurse and you can be the patient. We'll do surgery on you. Brain surgery most likely."

Vatsana could see that Souk was trying to think of something to say back to her. "Just wait," he finally muttered.

Vatsana laughed. She loved Souk, but it was fun to tease him sometimes. Especially because she could think up things to say to him that she hardly would to anyone else. Becky was the only other person that she could joke around with like that.

Their mother must have been half-listening to their conversation because she stopped working for just a minute and smiled at Souk and Vatsana. "I know you and your cousin will be good friends," she said to both of them in Lao. "Family always makes the best friends."

Vatsana finished her cereal, rinsed her bowl out, and set it down by the sink. She could see from the kitchen window that it was a cloudy day but it wasn't raining. It looked nice outside for a winter day and she felt kind of restless, so she decided to go for a walk.

"I'm going outside for a little bit," she told her mother.

"You have your watch?" her mother asked.

Vatsana smiled. Her mother didn't usually worry. Most of the time if little things went wrong, she would just laugh and say *"Bo pen nyang,"* which was the Lao way of saying "never mind." It was funny to see her being nervous today.

"I've got my watch," Vatsana assured her mother, "and I'll be back in plenty of time."

Vatsana put on her dark green winter jacket and light green wool hat and stuck her gloves into her pocket. Both her jacket and hat were new, and she liked the way she looked in them. Once she got outside, she was glad she'd decided to take a walk. She and Becky talked a lot when they walked together. They had great conversations on the way to and from school. But sometimes it felt good just walking alone.

It was easier to look at the sky when she was by herself. Today it was a chalky color but against the whiteness there were rainclouds in shades of lighter and darker gray. The rainclouds looked soft and furry at the edges.

Staring at the clouds made Vatsana feel peaceful. But she couldn't quite forget that Aunt Lavanny and Ketsy would be here soon. Maybe this would be the last time she would take a walk alone for a while. Her mother would want her to spend time with Ketsy and help her get used to living in the United States.

Her mother was so sure that she and Ketsy would be friends–just because they were cousins. That didn't make sense, Vatsana thought. She and Becky weren't related at all but they were good friends.

Vatsana looked at her watch and decided she'd better turn back. She walked a little bit faster now. Well, she'd try to be friends with Ketsy. And maybe after a long time—like by the time they were ready to get married—she and Ketsy would even feel like sisters.

They drove out to the airport in two cars—so there'd be plenty of room for everyone on the way back and for whatever bags Aunt Lavanny and Ketsy brought. Vatsana's father drove his car and Vyvone drove their mother's car, because she was in such a hurry to get to the airport that Vatsana's father was afraid she might have a wreck if she drove her own car.

Inside the airport terminal there were people standing in line to get tickets, people sitting or waiting or heading for their gates. Vatsana's father told Vyvone to check the arrival time of Aunt Lavanny's plane. "It's on time," Vyvone announced a couple of minutes later.

The plane wasn't due in for another half hour, but Vatsana's mother insisted that they should go to the gate anyway and wait. She ignored Souk's suggestion that they get ice cream cones first.

"The airport could be wrong," Vatsana's mother said. "Their plane could come in early and then they would have to wait there all alone when they arrived."

They all walked through the metal detecting machine and down the long corridor leading to the gate. Some other people were waiting there already, but Vatsana and Souk found seats facing the window where they could watch the planes taking off and landing.

At last a plane pulled in right in front of their window. A few minutes later, the passengers started coming out. There were mostly American passengers, and some Asians too. Vatsana scanned the faces of the passengers, trying to see if any of them looked like the pictures of her aunt Lavanny and her cousin Ketsy.

Vatsana's mother gave an excited cry. "It's them," she said in Lao. She walked quickly toward them, and the rest of the family followed.

Vatsana's mother and aunt Lavanny hugged each other. Then they were both smiling and talking at the same time. They were talking so fast in Lao that it was hard for Vatsana to understand exactly what they were saying.

A girl was standing next to Aunt Lavanny. It had to be Ketsy, Vatsana figured. The girl's eyes were downcast. She wasn't smiling the way Aunt Lavanny was. Instead she looked serious, and maybe a little scared.

Aunt Lavanny put her palms together beneath her chin and bowed to Vatsana's father. That was the Lao way to show respect for someone. *"Sa bai dee,"* she said.

Vatsana's father said, *"Sa bai dee,"* back to Aunt Lavanny. He smiled at her. "How are you? Are you tired from your trip?"

"A little tired," Aunt Lavanny said, smiling too. "We're lucky we could sleep on the plane." Aunt Lavanny was shorter than Vatsana's mother and on the plump side. She wore her hair pulled back behind her head in a bun, which mostly only the older Lao women did in the United States.

The Lao custom was that everybody would be introduced in order, with grown-ups first and children coming last. Pretty soon Aunt Lavanny put her hand on Ketsy. "This is your uncle. This is your aunt," she said to her. Ketsy pressed her palms together and bowed to Vatsana's father and mother. She looked a lot more graceful doing that than Vatsana felt she ever did.

Vatsana's mother looked at Vatsana, Souk, and Vyvone. "Say *sa bai dee* to your aunt," she said to them. Vatsana, Vyvone, and Souk bowed to Aunt Lavanny and said, *"Sa bai dee."* Vatsana felt stupid doing that in the middle of the airport with lots of other people around.

"You're so big now," Aunt Lavanny said to Vyvone. "You were only a little boy the last time I saw you."

Then she turned to Vatsana and Souk. "So finally I see my nephew and niece. Many times

I have prayed to Buddha that I would be able to know you more than just in letters."

Vatsana smiled back at Aunt Lavanny. She looked sideways at Ketsy, so it wouldn't seem like she was staring at her. Ketsy had long hair like Vatsana did, and she wore it tied back in a pony tail. She was slender and just a little shorter than Vatsana was, but her face was prettier, Vatsana decided.

Aunt Lavanny introduced Ketsy to Vatsana, Vyvone, and Souk. They all said "*Sa bai dee*" to each other, but nobody had to bow because they were all kids.

Ketsy smiled shyly at Vatsana, Souk, and Vyvone. "My mother told me about you many times," she said in Lao.

They all started walking toward the baggage area. Vatsana's mother, father, and aunt Lavanny were still talking to each other in Lao, and Vatsana saw a few people giving them curious glances as they passed.

"No time for ice cream now," she said in English to Souk in a loud voice, so the people around them would know that she and Souk weren't from another country like Aunt Lavanny and Ketsy.

Souk just scowled at her. He was only eight years old. Maybe he didn't care whether people knew he was an American.

5

"So this is your American house," Aunt Lavanny said when they got back from the airport. "It's so different from our family's home in Laos." She stared at the house a moment longer. Then she smiled. "But it's very nice."

They did have a good house, Vatsana thought. It was an older house with two stories, a front porch with an overhanging roof, and a fenced backyard where they planted a garden in the summertime. The creamy color the house was painted gave it a homey look.

Vatsana's father unlocked the front door and they went inside. Aunt Lavanny acted pretty nice, Vatsana decided. It was harder to tell about Ketsy though. She seemed kind of quiet.

They all sat down in the living room. "Are you hungry and thirsty after your trip?" Vatsana's mother asked Aunt Lavanny and Ketsy. Offering food to a guest was a Lao custom.

"Something to drink would be good," Aunt Lavanny said. "And maybe we could eat just a little bit." She laughed. "I think my stomach got smaller on the airplane."

"Come help me," Vatsana's mother said to Vatsana. She followed her mother into the kitchen. Before they left for the airport, Vatsana's mother had chopped up meat and vegetables and prepared sauces and spices. She was keeping rice warm in a rice cooker. Vatsana handed her mother the things she needed and cooked some noodles while her mother stir-fried the spices and meat and vegetables in her wok and heated up some soup. When the food was ready, Vatsana and her mother brought it out. There was a container of rice, a big bowl of noodles, soup, meat and vegetables, and sauces for dipping things in.

They sat on a mat around the low table and ate. When they finished eating, Aunt Lavanny asked Ketsy to bring one of their bags. Then Aunt Lavanny took out presents for everyone.

She gave Vatsana's father a shirt from Thailand. He grinned and held the shirt up against himself. *"Cop chai,"* he said, which meant "thank you" in Lao.

41

For Vatsana's mother there was a small statue of Buddha. "From our mother and me," Aunt Lavanny said. Vatsana's mother looked a little teary-eyed as she took the statue and thanked Aunt Lavanny.

Aunt Lavanny gave Souk and Vyvone fabric shoulder bags with Lao embroidery on them. In Laos, that was a good gift for boys, but Vatsana wondered what Souk and Vyvone would do with the bags in Portland.

Last of all, Aunt Lavanny took out a small, flat package for Vatsana. "Ketsy helped me choose this," she said to Vatsana.

Ketsy was watching her, Vatsana noticed. She unwrapped the package. Inside, there was a rectangular piece of fabric. It was a weaving with a geometrical design in shades of blue, green, pink, and yellow.

"We brought it with us from Laos," Aunt Lavanny said.

"*Cop chai,*" Vatsana said. She looked at the square of fabric again. It really was kind of pretty, and Ketsy had been nice to help pick it out. Maybe she could find some place to put it in her room.

Aunt Lavanny and Ketsy were both looking tired, but they said they couldn't sleep yet when Vatsana's mother asked them. So Vatsana's mother, father, and aunt Lavanny sat and talked for a while.

Vatsana's mother and aunt Lavanny had two older brothers who were living in France with their wives and children. They talked about them and also about their mother, Vatsana's grandmother, who had died a year ago. Since Aunt Lavanny was the youngest daughter, she had lived with her mother and father and taken care of both of them until they died.

After a while the little group began to talk about Laos. "The new government is easier on people now," Aunt Lavanny said. "They release more people from the re-education camps."

Those were like jails for people the new government didn't like, Vatsana knew. Ketsy's father had been in a re-education camp. He had been killed when a bomb hidden in the ground exploded as he was doing farm work. Vatsana remembered her mother crying when she read the letter Aunt Lavanny wrote about that.

It must have been hard for Ketsy to lose her father, Vatsana thought. Vatsana's father got really angry at her once in a while. But even then she always knew that he loved her.

All of a sudden Vatsana noticed that Ketsy was looking at her. When Ketsy saw Vatsana looking back at her, she smiled a little, as if she were embarrassed. Then she lowered her eyes. Either she was just trying to be polite, Vatsana decided, or she was really shy.

"Do you want to come see my room?" Vatsana asked Ketsy. She felt sorry for Ketsy, so that made it easier not to be shy herself.

Ketsy followed Vatsana up the stairs. Vatsana showed Ketsy where the bathroom was, and pointed out her parents' room and the room that Souk and Vyvone shared. Her own room was the smallest bedroom of the three, and it looked even smaller with the bed Ketsy would sleep on next to Vatsana's own bed.

"This is a nice room," Ketsy said. Then she didn't say anything else. Vatsana sat down on one of the beds and Ketsy sat on the other one. The bureau they were going to share was squashed between the beds.

Neither of them said anything for a minute or two. Vatsana was trying to come up with something to talk about. They couldn't go on sitting there as if they'd been turned into statues.

"Are you glad you came to the United States?" Vatsana asked Ketsy. It wasn't exactly an inspired question, but she couldn't think of anything else to say.

"My mother and I were both thankful to leave the refugee camp," Ketsy said. Her voice sounded stiff. "And I wanted to be with my American family."

Even though you've never met any of us before? Vatsana wondered. But she didn't say that to Ketsy. Ketsy was being polite and so could she, although her mother said sometimes that American children didn't have good manners.

"Do you think you'll like it here?" Vatsana asked.

Ketsy looked a little surprised. Maybe she wasn't used to being asked so many questions.

"I don't know about the United States yet," Ketsy said in a quiet voice. "I always thought America was so far away. And now I'm here in America."

That was the main difference between them, Vatsana thought. To her, Laos was the place that was far away. A faraway, different land, which her parents still thought of as home.

Vatsana wasn't sure what to do or say next. Even if she and Ketsy were cousins, they were really strangers. Maybe Ketsy would rather go back downstairs and be with her mother. But Ketsy didn't say anything about what she wanted to do.

"Do you know any English?" Vatsana asked Ketsy.

"Just a little," Ketsy said. "In the refugee camp we studied English, but only after we knew we were coming to the United States."

This was going to be hard, Vatsana thought. She tried not to let her discouragement show on her face. Ketsy was too tired now from her trip, but sometime soon Vatsana would have to start teaching her English and about life in the United States.

On Monday morning, Vatsana got dressed quietly because Ketsy was still sleeping. She and Aunt Lavanny were really tired from their long trip, Vatsana's mother told her.

After breakfast, Vatsana headed for Becky's house so the two of them could walk to school together. She was glad that Ketsy wasn't coming to school with her today. First Ketsy had to get her shots. Then, at least for a while, Ketsy would be in the Newcomer's Program, which was at a different school. That meant Vatsana wouldn't have to deal with any of the kids being weird to Ketsy or making nasty cracks about her. She'd seen some kids in her school do that with new refugee kids.

47

Becky came right out when Vatsana rang the doorbell. "So what are they like?" Betsy asked when she and Vatsana were halfway down the block. "Your relatives, I mean."

"They're okay," Vatsana said. "My aunt is pretty nice. She looks a lot like my mother. It's kind of neat to see them together."

"What about Ketsy?" Becky asked.

Vatsana hesitated. "She's awfully quiet. Kind of shy maybe. And polite all the time. We're sharing the same room, but I can't think of much to talk about with her."

Becky gave Vatsana a sympathetic look. "I bet she's got culture shock. They say most people get that if they move to a different part of the world. You have to get used to a whole new way of doing things, and all that makes you feel kind of off balance for a while." Becky staggered down the sidewalk a few steps, as if she were drunk, to imitate a person with culture shock.

Vatsana laughed. It was encouraging to think that Ketsy might get over her culture shock like you got over a case of the flu. Since they had to share a room after all, it would be a lot easier if Ketsy didn't act like she was scared most of the time.

"I guess she's pretty scared right now," Vatsana said.

"Think how you or I would feel if we were all of a sudden living in her country," Becky said. She grinned. "Of course, that would be a lot easier for you than for me."

Vatsana shook her head. "That's not true. Laos is like a foreign country to me. I wasn't even born yet when my parents escaped from there."

"Yeah," Becky said. "I see what you mean." She waved at a girl they knew who was just about to cross the street. "Anyway, I'd like to meet Ketsy. I bet once she gets over her culture shock, she can tell us some really interesting stuff about her country."

Every now and then Vatsana realized what a good friend Becky was. This was one of those moments. She didn't know why, but it made her feel good inside that Becky wanted to meet Ketsy.

She smiled at Becky. "Do you want to come over today after school?"

"Sure, Becky said. That'll be great."

Mr. Hansen's math class was about as usual that Monday. Kids talking while Mr. Hansen tried to talk. Kids who hadn't done their homework trying to fake it the best they could. The class was going about twice as slowly as it should be through the math book because kids kept interrupting Mr. Hansen's explanations to ask him questions.

Some of the kids were acting pretty dumb, Vatsana thought. She didn't like Mr. Hansen much either. But she wanted to learn the math. When the kids finally let Mr. Hansen talk, his explanations of the math problems were easy to understand. That was the one good thing about Mr. Hansen.

The class was almost over when Tom Connors poked Vatsana. A moment later, he slipped a folded piece of paper onto her desk. Maybe the note was from somebody else and Tom was just passing it along, Vatsana hoped. She unfolded the piece of paper. "Hey Teacher's Pet," the note said. "How come you're not showing off today?"

As soon as she read the note, Vatsana crumpled it up. But she didn't turn around and look at Tom Connors or say anything to him. Doing that would just let him know that he was bothering her.

The class was over soon after. She had her science and advisory classes next, and then school was done for the day. Vatsana tried to forget about Tom Connors as she headed for the locker she and Becky shared. She had better things to think about. Ketsy didn't know it, but she and Becky were going to meet each other this afternoon. That was a little scary, but kind of exciting too.

Vatsana and Becky walked to Vatsana's house along one of their usual routes, down side streets mostly, past some of their favorite houses. Like the big old house with a bell-shaped shingle roof over the porch and a weathervane on top. That same house had a tall madrone tree in the backyard with a gracefully curved bronze-colored trunk.

Souk was watching TV in the living room at Vatsana's house. "Mom came home from work so she could take Ketsy to get her shots for school," he told Vatsana.

"I guess they'll be back soon," Vatsana said to Becky. She got a plate of cookies and then the two of them went upstairs.

"It looks kind of crowded in here," Becky said as she looked at the extra bed Vatsana's father had manged to fit into the room.

"Yeah," Vatsana agreed. She made a face. "It's going to be weird not having my own room anymore."

"Maybe once Ketsy starts school she'll get home later than you do. Then you can have some time for yourself," Becky said. "I go bananas if I don't get time alone in my room most days," Becky added.

Vatsana grinned. "Maybe I'll go bananas too. I'll turn all yellow with brown spots and nobody'll know who I am."

She and Becky were both laughing when they heard the front doorbell ring. "That's probably Aunt Lavanny and Ketsy," Vatsana said.

A couple of minutes later Ketsy walked into the room. She came in slowly, a shy expression on her face.

"*Sa bai dee,*" Vatsana said to her, using the Lao expression for hello. Even at home, she usually just said hi or hello. But Ketsy looked so shy that, again, Vatsana felt sorry for her.

"This is my friend Becky," she said to Ketsy in Lao.

Becky gave Ketsy a big smile. "Tell her I'm really glad to meet her," she told Vatsana.

When Vatsana translated that, the uncertain expression on Ketsy's face changed to a shy smile. "I'm happy too," she said in Lao.

The three of them were quiet for a moment. This translation business didn't make for an easy conversation, Vatsana thought. Especially since her Lao speaking wasn't super good. At least it was better than her reading and writing in Lao.

"Ask her how she likes Portland," Becky said.

Ketsy didn't answer right away. "I see so many new things," she finally said. "All the streets and houses and the stores look different. And everywhere I see so many cars." Then she stopped talking and looked down at the rug.

"Almost everybody has their own car in America," Becky said. "Except kids of course." She smiled sympathetically when Ketsy looked back at her and Vatsana. "I bet it's hard to be in a whole new place all of a sudden. Vatsana and I will help you with stuff like learning English."

Vatsana translated again. Turning her head from Becky to Ketsy and trying to think in two languages made her feel like a ping-pong ball. But she was glad that Becky had offered to help teach Ketsy English. With the two of them helping her, they could give her a headstart on the English classes she'd have once she started school. Besides, with Becky helping too, it all would be a lot more fun.

"Let's start teaching her right now," Becky said enthusiastically. Becky always had a lot of energy for new projects.

"Okay," Vatsana said. Ketsy knew a little English already from the lessons she'd had in the refugee camp, which ought to make teaching her easier.

One of the things Vatsana liked so much about Becky was that when she got ready to do something, she plowed right into it instead of sitting around and thinking about it as Vatsana often did.

"I'm from the United States," she said, pointing to herself. She smiled encouragingly at Ketsy. "What country are you from?" she asked her.

Ketsy looked blank for a moment. Then she smiled too, as if she suddenly remembered the English she'd learned in the refugee camp. "My name is Ketsy. I'm from Laos."

Becky grinned at Vatsana. "See. I told you we could do it. We'll have her speaking English in no time at all."

All the rest of that week, Becky came over to Vatsana's house after school and the two of them helped Ketsy with her English.

Actually, Becky helped more than she did, Vatsana decided. Of course, she did all the translating. But Becky was the one who was really patient with Ketsy. Becky helped explain how English verbs worked and how they changed from present to past to future. Vatsana knew all that would be hard for Ketsy, because Lao verbs didn't work that way. But Vatsana still found herself getting irritated sometimes when Ketsy didn't catch on right away or when she forgot something they had already taught her.

Becky was also the one who was better at getting Ketsy to talk about herself. Maybe it should have been the other way around, since Vatsana was Ketsy's cousin. But sometimes Ketsy kept her eyes downcast and wouldn't say very much. It was probably lucky that either one of them could get Ketsy talking sometimes.

"How did you escape from Laos?" Becky asked Ketsy one day. Vatsana translated the question into Lao.

"We hid along the Mekong River until dark," Ketsy said in a soft voice. "My mother paid money to a man with a boat so he would take us across the river to Thailand. We had to be very quiet so no one would hear us. If the soldiers knew we were escaping, they might shoot us."

"That's terrible!" Becky said after Vatsana translated. "What happened after that?" she asked Ketsy a moment later.

Ketsy's face was serious. "When we got to Thailand, we gave some of the Thai people pieces of gold so they would let us stay in Thailand and let us into the refugee camp. If we didn't give them gold, they would send us back to Laos and maybe beat us up."

"That sounds really scary," Becky said to Ketsy. "I think you and your mother were brave to escape like that."

"It was the only way we could leave our country," Ketsy said.

"Your family escaped like that too, didn't they?" Becky asked Vatsana.

"My father was a helicopter pilot in the air force," Vatsana said. "So all he had to do was to fly his helicopter to Thailand. But my mother had to cross the Mekong River with Vyvone."

"I guess you were lucky to be born here," Becky said.

Vatsana nodded. She did feel lucky. It made her feel more like she belonged here in Portland. No matter what her mother said about missing pieces, Vatsana knew that all of the pieces of her life were here.

Vatsana's mother was pleased that Vatsana and Becky were spending every afternoon together with Ketsy. "Becky's a good friend," she said to Vatsana, "and you're a good cousin to Ketsy."

Aunt Lavanny and Becky would always smile at each other, even though Aunt Lavanny only knew a few words of English and Becky could only say "hello" and "thank you" in Lao. One afternoon, when Becky, Vatsana, Ketsy, and Aunt Lavanny were all sitting together in the living room, Aunt Lavanny put down her sewing and said that she had a story to tell them.

"The Buddha sent a boy down to the earth," Aunt Lavanny began. Vatsana translated that into English. "The boy was born into a rich family. In fact, his father was a king. When the boy was born, the people saw that his skin was black—the way a crow's feathers are black. The boy looked different from anybody else, and so most of the people thought he was ugly, and they were afraid of him. The boy's father said they would get a fortune teller to come and tell what the boy's future would be.

When the fortune teller came, he said the boy was evil. He told the family to send the boy away.

The father believed what the fortune teller said because he was scared by how different the boy looked. So the father built a boat and made a house on top of the boat. He put food and water in the boat. Then he put the boy into it and let the boat drift along on the river.

The boy stayed on the river, all alone, until he was sixteen years old. Then one day his boat reached an island. His boat ran aground on the shores of the island and the boy left the boat. He walked around the island, exploring it, until he came to a house. It was built up on stilts, like most Lao houses are, and there was a ladder leading up to the part where people would live.

The boy climbed up the ladder and went inside the house. There was a shady porch on the front, with a big jar of water for drinking. The boy drank some of the cool water and sat there and waited, hoping someone would come.

At the end of the day an old woman climbed up the house ladder. It was her house and she lived there all alone. When the boy told her his story, though, she felt sorry for him. Even though she thought he was strange looking, she told him he could stay with her and help her work in the sugarcane fields on her island.

The old woman worked for a king in a nearby town. Every week she made a necklace with flowers from her garden and brought it over to the princess, the oldest daughter of the king.

The boy helped the old woman make the necklaces of flowers, and one day, when the old woman wasn't watching him, he put a message into the necklace he made. He told the princess that he was a boy living alone and that he was in love with her. If she wanted to see him, he wrote, she should come to the old woman's house.

The old woman took the flower necklace to the princess and the princess read the boy's message. Then she asked the old woman many questions. She wanted to know who the boy was and what he looked like. She insisted that the old woman help her make arrangements to see the boy. The old woman agreed because the girl was a princess. But the old woman was afraid. If the king found out, he would blame her for letting his daughter meet a strange boy. And if people made trouble for the king, he would chop their heads off.

The next day the old woman helped the princess come to the island. She told the boy to hide behind a bamboo wall of her house. So he hid himself, but he looked at the princess through a little hole in the bamboo wall. As soon as the old woman moved away, the boy talked to the princess. He told her how beautiful she was and how much he loved her.

The boy's voice was so musical and his words were so sweet that the princess wanted to see him. But the boy wouldn't come out from behind the wall. After a while, the princess went away.

The next day the boy met some other boys his age, who were his friends. They all went to the house of the princess and stood outside. The boy blew into the bamboo pipes of his *khene* to make a song for the girl. When the girl heard the song, she ran outside to see who was playing it.

As soon as the girl saw the boy, she was afraid of him because his skin was as dark as a crow's feathers. She'd never seen anyone like him before, but she still couldn't stop herself from falling in love with him. Because even though the girl and boy didn't know it, they had come down from the sky, where they had been husband and wife.

When the king discovered that she was in love with the boy, he was angry at first. He didn't want the princess to marry the boy because he was poor and didn't have any parents. Also, the king thought the boy was too different from other people.

About that time the boy's parents found out that he was still alive and was living on an island with an old woman. The boy's parents felt sorry now that they had sent him away. They decided that the fortune teller had been wrong. Just because the boy was different, that didn't mean he was evil or ugly.

The boy's parents told the king that the boy was their son. Now the king was happy because the boy's father was a king too.

Some of the people still thought the boy was too strange. But when they saw how much the princess loved him, they began to see the boy with new eyes. They saw what a fine boy he was.

The boy and the girl got married then. The girl's father had three other daughters, but the boy's parents had no other children, so the couple went to live with them. The boy and girl loved each other and everyone was very happy."

"That's the end of the story," Aunt Lavanny said. She smiled at all her listeners. "My grandmother told my mother that story and my mother told me. Now I'm telling you so you'll remember for your own children someday."

Vatsana and Becky grinned at each other. They weren't even in high school yet, Vatsana thought, so it was funny to think about having children. She liked the story though. Her aunt Lavanny was a good storyteller. And it was neat the way the girl fell in love with the boy even though most people thought he looked weird. So maybe she would tell it to her own children some day.

Becky looked at her watch. "I better get home and help my mom with dinner. Tell your aunt Lavanny that I really liked her story," she said to Vatsana. "I'll see you tomorrow morning."

After Becky left, Vatsana went upstairs to her room. She was hoping that she could have a few minutes alone, but Ketsy came into the room a moment later.

Maybe Ketsy just wanted to get something, Vatsana thought. She lay down on her bed, opened a library book, and tried to look as if she were reading it.

Ketsy didn't take the hint though. She sat down on her own bed so she was facing Vatsana. "I've heard my mother tell that story many times," Ketsy said in Lao. "But today I feel sad when I listen to it."

Vatsana took her eyes off the book. Ketsy wasn't crying or anything but she did look sad. "How come? The story had a happy ending."

Ketsy's eyebrows drew together, and Vatsana could see she was thinking. "I know the story is happy at the end," she said finally, "but the boy must be very unhappy first. Because everybody thinks he's so different."

Ketsy looked at Vatsana, then looked away. "I think I'm the different one here," she said. "In the United States I feel like that boy sometimes."

"You don't look anything like a crow," Vatsana said. She smiled at Ketsy, but Ketsy didn't smile back. "I see what you mean," Vatsana said a moment later. "I guess you are different. But after a while you'll know more about living here."

"I know I need to learn a lot," Ketsy said. Her voice was quiet and a little shaky. "But maybe I'll always be different inside."

8

When Becky and Vatsana waited for lunch the next Monday, they ended up standing in line right behind David Stafford, who sat near both of them in Mrs. O'Malia's class. David had light brown hair and brown eyes, and Vatsana thought he was awfully good looking. Today he was wearing a sweatshirt with a picture of a seal on it.

David smiled at Becky and Vatsana. "Ready for another great school lunch?"

"We just can't stay away from them," Becky said.

David laughed. "How'd you do on today's writing?" Mrs. O'Malia had asked them to write a composition in class about whether they

64

thought they would have liked to live in the Middle Ages.

"We hope okay," Becky said.

"Me too," David agreed. Actually, he was one of the best writers in the class. Whenever he read his papers in class, they were really good.

The three of them reached the food part of the line. Pizza was one of the choices today, and they all got that. "Want to sit with us?" Becky asked David.

"Sure," David said.

Mostly Becky and David talked while they ate. David was really nice, but Vatsana still felt shy with him, the way she did with most boys.

"Did you know that David's family sponsored a Vietnamese refugee family a few years ago?" Becky asked Vatsana.

Vatsana shook her head. She hadn't known that.

"That was pretty interesting," David said. "There were two boys in the family and one of them, Dung, was around my age. He sure had had a different life from mine." David looked thoughtful. "Dung and I got to be good friends anyway. His family moved up to Seattle, but I still get to see him once in a while."

Maybe Ketsy and she would be good friends too, Vatsana thought. She didn't know how soon that was going to happen though.

"Vatsana's aunt and cousin just came over from Laos," Becky said to David. "Her family sponsored them."

"That's great," David said. "They're lucky to have family here."

"I don't think they could have come if our family wasn't here," Vatsana said. "My father says that these days not very many refugees are being admitted to the United States." She looked at David. He wasn't laughing at her or anything. Instead he seemed genuinely interested.

Their lunch period was almost over so they cleaned up their lunches and got their books. Becky had her art class after lunch, and Vatsana had Mr. Hansen's math class, as usual.

Mr. Hansen started going over the homework at the beginning of the class. Vatsana only half listened because she was still thinking about David. He was the nicest boy she knew in their school, and it felt good to talk with him. She liked the way he'd told her about being friends with the boy from Vietnam.

Mr. Hansen had a few students do problems at the board. Most of the kids he called on did okay, but Tom Connors got red in the face when he couldn't finish his problem correctly. His shoulders were hunched and he had an angry expression on his face when he went back to his seat.

Mr. Hansen didn't call on Vatsana, which was fine with her. In the last part of the class he gave them a quiz, and he sat at his desk and stared at them while they took it. At least Mr. Hansen didn't let kids cheat on the quizzes he gave. That was one other good thing about him.

The class handed in their quizzes just before the bell rang. Then one more of Mr. Hansen's math classes was over.

Vatsana was standing in the hallway outside Mr. Hansen's room, rearranging her books, when Tom Connors came up to her. He looked mad. Probably he hadn't done very well on the quiz, Vatsana figured.

"Hey chink," Tom said in a low voice. "Bet you're sorry you didn't get called on today, huh? You didn't have a chance to show the rest of us how smart all you chinks are."

Vatsana just stared at him. Tom had been a jerk to her all year, but he'd never called her a name like "chink" before. "I'm not Chinese," she finally said.

"Is that right?" Tom said, making it sound like that was some kind of big joke. "I guess I could have figured that out, huh?" His voice was low enough that no one else could hear them. "You must be a gook then."

Vatsana didn't say anything. The way Tom Connors was looking at her scared her a little.

"Well, see you around, gook," he said. Then he walked off down the hall.

It was almost time for the next period to start. Vatsana started walking slowly toward her science class. She was really mad at Tom Connors, madder than she'd ever been before. But she felt kind of embarrassed too. Like it was somehow her fault that he'd called her a gook. Like being a gook wasn't as good as being an American.

She could report Tom to one of her teachers and he'd get in trouble for sure. But then he'd just get back at her some way. All she wanted was for Tom to leave her alone. Probably the best thing to do was to go on trying to ignore him.

Deciding that didn't leave her feeling very good inside. But she didn't know what else to do.

That Saturday Vatsana's mother and father were giving a party for Aunt Lavanny and Ketsy. People were going to come about twelve o'clock, so that morning Vatsana's mother started to make a special arrangement of fruit and flowers in the living room.

The Lao word for what she was making was *pa kouan*. It was a decoration Lao people made for a ceremony called a *baci*—which sounded like "bah-see." People had a *baci* if someone made a long trip, when a baby was one month old, when people got married, and at other special times.

"Bring me the white tablecloth," Vatsana's mother said. When Vatsana brought it, her mother draped the cloth over a low, round table made of bamboo. Then she arranged bunches of bananas and some apples and mangoes around the table and at its base. She placed colored rice cakes and a few hard boiled eggs in with the fruit.

Vatsana had always liked to look at the silver bowl that her mother put in the center of the table. It was the one her mother usually brought to the Buddhist temple. The bowl was made of shiny silver, and around the outside it had raised designs.

Inside the bowl, her mother put long stemmed flowers, long orange and yellow candles, and sticks of incense. Finally, she draped pieces of white cotton string from long sticks on either side of the decoration.

When Vatsana's mother was finished making the *pa kouan*, she smiled at Vatsana and Ketsy. "Sometime soon I'll teach both of you to make this too. So you can do it for your own family some day." The *pa kouan* looked nice, but Vatsana wasn't sure whether she would make one or not if she had a family of her own. She didn't say that to her mother though. She didn't want to get her mother started on a lecture about how important it was for them to keep their Lao customs.

"Now," Vatsana's mother said to Vatsana, "I need a few things from the store. So you and Ketsy can walk to the store together."

"Okay," Vatsana said. It was fine with her. She liked the idea of getting out of the house for a little bit before the *baci* ceremony started.

On the way to the store, Vatsana walked quickly, but Ketsy kept up with her easily. "Is Becky coming to the *baci* ceremony?" Ketsy asked in Lao.

"Uh-uh," Vatsana said. She didn't feel like explaining.

"The *baci* ceremony is beautiful," Ketsy said, "I think Becky would like it."

"Becky's busy today. So maybe another time," Vatsana muttered. She walked even faster. She'd told Becky about the *baci* ceremony yesterday, but Becky had already made plans to go shopping with her mother. She could have invited Becky earlier of course. Maybe she should have.

But she wasn't going to tell Ketsy all that. Becky was Vatsana's best friend, and it was her business whether she invited Becky or not. Besides, why did Ketsy care so much whether Becky was there? Maybe Ketsy would rather have Becky there than Vatsana.

Ketsy didn't say anything more about Becky. They got milk and bread and a couple of other things at the store. Then they walked home quickly. By the time they got there, it was time for them to get dressed for the *baci* ceremony.

Just this year Vatsana's mother had decided Vatsana was old enough to wear a *sin*. The *sin* was the traditional Lao skirt. Lao people pronounced the name for it so it sounded like "seen" in English.

Vatsana liked wearing American clothes a lot more than Lao clothes, but she did think the *sin* looked pretty. And it made her feel grown-up to wear it. Hers was wine-colored with gold and silver embroidery around the bottom, and it went all the way from her waist to her ankles.

Ketsy was wearing a *sin* also. The two girls helped each other wrap the long pieces of fabric around their hips and legs and then tuck them in at the waist. That was one advantage of sharing a room with her cousin, Vatsana had to admit. They could help each other sometimes.

Around noon, the guests started arriving. Aside from her aunt Lavanny and Ketsy, Vatsana's mother and father didn't have any other family in Portland. But they knew many Lao people here, and they had invited their friends to meet Aunt Lavanny and Ketsy.

The men were wearing American clothes, but most of the women and a lot of the older girls were wearing the *sin*. "You look so much like cousins," one of the women told Vatsana and Ketsy. That made Vatsana feel good for a moment. But she still thought that she and Ketsy looked different. She was skinnier than

Ketsy and Ketsy was prettier. Plus Ketsy didn't walk around as if she was always about to bump into something.

A few more guests were still coming. Everybody left their shoes at the door, as was the Lao custom. Mostly the men stayed in one room and talked or stood outside and smoked. The women stayed together in another room.

Vatsana was glad to see a girl around her own age named Alida come into the house. Like many of the other Lao kids there, Alida lived in a different neighborhood and went to a different school. But she was always friendly and Vatsana liked seeing her at Lao parties or religious celebrations.

"Hi," Alida said. "Is that your cousin? How long has she been here?"

"Ketsy's only been here a week. She and my aunt Lavanny came last Sunday."

Vatsana spoke English when she introduced Ketsy to Alida. She and the other Lao-American kids usually spoke English to each other, and she figured Ketsy could understand that much by now. After that they switched to Lao so Ketsy wouldn't feel left out. That was kind of a pain, but Vatsana knew it would be rude to talk in English when Ketsy still understood so little.

When everyone had arrived at the party, as many people as possible made a big circle around the *pa kouan*. They sat on mats on the floor with their legs tucked under them. Vatsana's mother and father, Vatsana and Vyvone, and Aunt Lavanny and Ketsy were all in the circle. Souk was too young to sit still, so he was playing upstairs with some of his friends.

Vatsana's father started the *baci* ceremony by lighting the candles and the sticks of incense on the *pa kouan*. An old Lao man pressed his hands together in front of his chest and everybody else did the same thing. Then the old man said some prayers. They were in Lao, but Vatsana couldn't understand many of the words. That was why, as usual, she thought that the prayers were boring.

Vatsana's mother had told Vatsana what the prayers were about. The traditional Lao belief was that everyone had 32 souls, and the souls could wander away. So the prayers were designed to bring together all the souls of the people being honored.

It was kind of a funny idea, Vatsana thought. She pictured different parts of Aunt Lavanny and Ketsy wandering away and returning. Maybe that was like the missing part of herself her mother had warned Vatsana about.

After the prayers were finished, the old man tied a piece of cotton string around Aunt Lavanny's wrist. "May you be happy in

America," he said to her. Aunt Lavanny pressed her hands together and said *"cop chai,"* which meant "thank you."

Vatsana's mother and father and many other people tied more strings around Aunt Lavanny's wrists and gave her more good wishes. "May you have a happy and long life," some people said to her.

The old man tied a string around Ketsy's wrist and made a wish for her too. Then other people tied strings and made wishes for her until she had bracelets of white cotton strings around her wrists.

Vatsana felt a little silly doing it but she took cotton strings and tied them around Aunt Lavanny's and Ketsy's wrists. "May you learn English quickly," she said to Ketsy. You could make any wish you wanted to, and Vatsana figured that was a good one.

Finally the ceremony was over and it was time to eat. Most of the time Vatsana preferred American food to Lao food. But she did like some Lao dishes, and she was really hungry by now.

Vatsana's mother and some of the other women brought out big platters of food and people sat on mats on the floor around the dishes of food. Everybody sat around the platters of food and helped themselves. They took balls of sticky rice from woven bamboo holders and dipped the rice in spicy sauces or picked up pieces of meat or greens with it. They ate bowls of noodles and soup as well.

Vatsana was sitting with Ketsy, Alida, and Tara, a girl about their age who had come to the United States six years ago. They talked in English a little but mostly in Lao, because of Ketsy.

All of a sudden Vatsana wondered what it would be like if Becky were here. What would Becky think about this party and all the Lao people and Lao food and the *baci* ceremony especially?

Ketsy thought the *baci* ceremony was beautiful. Vatsana wouldn't go that far, but she did think the *pa kouan* was pretty. And she liked the idea of giving good wishes to people. That was kind of nice.

If she had invited Becky sooner, maybe she would have come. But what if Becky had thought all this was too foreign, too strange and different?

Becky wasn't like Tom Connors. Vatsana knew that for sure. She wouldn't laugh or call people names or anything like that. Maybe Becky would just have figured the *baci* ceremony was boring, the way Vatsana thought a lot of Lao customs were.

Alida and Tara noticed how quiet Vatsana was and asked her why. "Maybe she's thinking about her boyfriend," Alida said, and they all laughed.

Mostly Vatsana stopped thinking about Becky after that. But part of her was still wondering what it would have been like if Becky had been at the party with them.

Vatsana wondered if Mrs. O'Malia had some kind of ESP, because the Monday after the *baci* ceremony, Mrs. O'Malia talked to the class about special times. "Every country has important events which groups of people participate in," she explained. "Like Christmas, the Fourth of July, Thanksgiving, weddings and funerals."

"What about basketball games?" one boy said.

Mrs. O'Malia laughed along with the class. "Those can be special too," she agreed.

Mrs. O'Malia waited until the class was quieter. "Today we're going to do some more writing," she told the class. "I want you to choose a special event you've taken part in and tell me what it was like."

A few of the kids made faces, but nobody complained too much. Pretty soon most kids were busy writing.

Vatsana knew she couldn't write about Christmas. Since her family was Buddhist, they never celebrated Christmas. Her family didn't do that much for other American holidays either, even though she wished they would. She thought for a moment more, and then decided to write about the *baci* ceremony. She didn't know if Mrs. O'Malia would be interested in reading about that, but a *baci* ceremony was definitely one kind of special event. Plus it was the only idea that Vatsana had.

Describing the *baci* ceremony was pretty easy. Vatsana wrote about the *pa kouan*, and tying the cotton strings, and all that stuff. Before she knew it, Mrs. O'Malia told them to stop writing and she collected their papers.

"What'd you write about?" Becky asked after class.

"A Lao ceremony," Vatsana said. She still felt a little weird about not inviting Becky sooner, so she didn't feel like explaining.

"I wrote about a bat mitzvah," Becky said. "Boys have bar mitzvahs but Jewish girls have bat mitzvahs after they're twelve years old to show that they're women now." She put her hands on her hips. "I've had one already, so I guess that makes me a real woman."

Vatsana and Becky were laughing about that as they lined up for the cafeteria. When they had bought their lunches and were looking for a place to sit, David Stafford waved at them and pointed to empty seats at his table. He was sitting with another boy, Seth Owen, and a couple of girls, Pat Carter and Laura Chin. All of the students were in some of Vatsana's classes.

Except for Becky of course, Vatsana didn't know any of the other kids very well, so she sat and listened as they talked. When she was alone with Becky, she had a lot to say, but with a bunch of kids it was easier to be quiet.

David was talking about last weekend. "My whole family went cross-country skiing. I was having a great time until I fell into a tree well and my sister had to help dig me out."

David grinned at Vatsana. "I bet that never happened to you. You look like the graceful type."

Vatsana felt her face get hot. She shook her head. "I've never been skiing." She didn't think David was right about her being the graceful type either, even though she wished that she were.

"Not even once?" David asked. "That's practically un-Oregonian." The way he smiled at her reminded her of Souk, who was almost always in a happy mood.

In math class that Monday, Mr. Hansen gave them back the quizzes they'd taken on Friday. He usually got all their papers back to them pretty quickly, which Vatsana liked even though she still didn't like him as a teacher.

Vatsana couldn't help looking pleased when her own quiz came back with 100 percent written in red ink at the top. Then she noticed Tom Connors watching her and she stopped smiling. But she saw the angry expression on Tom's face when he looked at his own paper and the way he stuffed it into the back of his folder.

Maybe what happened later was because of the math quizzes they got back. Or maybe Tom had been planning on doing what he did anyway. When Vatsana thought about it afterward, she wasn't sure.

Becky had a dentist appointment after school, so she couldn't come over to Vatsana's house that afternoon. High clouds covered the sky, but it wasn't raining and the air felt warm, so Vatsana enjoyed the walk home. She hadn't gotten much time alone lately and she missed that.

Spring was coming quickly in Oregon, Mr. Goldberg, her science teacher, had said. Vatsana walked mainly on side streets, and in some of the front yards she passed she saw purple and yellow crocuses blooming. Next to them were the spearlike leaves of daffodils.

She didn't notice Tom Connors until she was about halfway home. He didn't say anything or look directly at her. He just kept on walking toward her. When they were almost even with each other, Tom stopped.

Vatsana tried to just ignore him and go around him. But Tom moved so she couldn't do that. He stood in the middle of the sidewalk, blocking Vatsana's way.

He was smiling at her, but it was more of a smirk than a smile. His smile scared Vatsana, but she didn't want him to know that.

"I guess you're surprised to see me, huh?" Tom said. "I know where you and your chink family live." He folded his arms across his chest. "That's right, I forgot. It's your gook family, isn't it?"

"We're from Laos," Vatsana said, but Tom acted as if he hadn't heard. He wasn't smiling anymore. Instead he had a mean look on his face.

"You gooks all think you're so smart," Tom said. "You think it's just great that you found a way to get into this country. I bet you even think that everybody in this country is glad to have more of you gooks."

"Some people are," Vatsana started to say, trying to keep her voice steady. Then she stopped. There was a lump in her throat and she felt as though she might start to cry. Anyway, she couldn't talk to Tom. She knew he wasn't going to listen to her.

She edged sideways and backwards. She just wanted to get away from Tom. But he stepped forward so that she still had to face him. Her back was against a low stone wall which fronted one of the houses.

"My dad told me all about you gooks," Tom hissed. "You killed some of his buddies in Vietnam. So don't think you can come over here and act like you're just as good as Americans."

Vatsana stared at Tom. His reddish eyebrows were drawn together and his face was flushed. She could feel so much hate coming from him that it stunned her.

He stared back at her for what seemed like a long time. They were standing close together now, almost face to face. "You gooks make me sick," he said.

He turned on his heels and stomped away. Vatsana just stood there, watching his receding figure. Her throat felt knotted up. She felt as if she could cry and throw up at the same time.

Slowly, she started walking again. Her mother got off from work around this time and she would probably worry if Vatsana wasn't at home. Walking helped anyway. She watched the squares of pavement and the lines between them go past one after another. It made the tight hurting feeling in her chest feel a little better.

Tom Connors hated her even though she'd never done anything to him. He thought she was a bad person just because her parents were from Laos. She felt a few tears spilling over now and running down her cheeks. She hated Tom Connors. She hated him just as much as he hated her.

She walked another block. She was getting closer to home now. But she couldn't stop thinking about what Tom Connors had said.

Tom must think all Asians were bad people. He must think she was ugly and different looking just like the boy in Aunt Lavanny's story.

It didn't make any sense. She didn't know why Tom would think that way. Her family wasn't even Vietnamese. Her father had been in the Lao air force, but he hadn't fought against the Americans. He hadn't killed any of Tom's father's buddies.

So why would Tom hate her? The question burned itself into her mind as she walked the rest of the way home. There was still that hurting feeling inside her. But part of her mind kept separate from the hurt and kept trying to understand.

The first thing Vatsana thought when she woke up the next morning was that she didn't want to go to school that day. She didn't want to see Tom Connors, or any of the other kids at school. She wasn't even sure that she wanted to see Becky.

Her mother stuck her head into the bedroom to be sure she and Ketsy were awake. Ketsy was already partly dressed, and Vatsana's mother smiled at her. "Hurry up," she said to Vatsana.

Vatsana sat up in bed. She still had the blankets pulled around her. "You look tired this morning. Did you have bad dreams?" Ketsy asked in Lao.

"I'm okay," Vatsana snapped. She forced herself to get out of bed. What business was it of Ketsy's what kind of dreams she had?

"Sometimes I dream I'm escaping from Laos and the soldiers catch me," Ketsy said.

"Oh yeah?" Vatsana muttered. She started putting on her school clothes. Why was Ketsy talking about her dreams all of a sudden? Especially this morning. She didn't feel like talking to anyone right now.

Ketsy didn't say anything more. Vatsana went to the bathroom and got washed up. Then she stuffed her schoolbooks into her backpack and went downstairs. She did feel tired this morning, tired and slow, as if her muscles and bones were moving in slow motion. Maybe she was getting sick, she thought hopefully. But she didn't think she could convince her mother of that.

"We're going to have a party at school today," Souk said. "It's for a girl's birthday."

Ketsy looked surprised. "In Laos," she told Souk, "we only study at school. We don't have parties there."

Souk and Ketsy kept on talking to each other, but Vatsana was quiet. She slowly ate some of her breakfast even though she didn't feel hungry.

"You must have got up on the wrong side of bed," her mother said to Vatsana in English.

Usually Vatsana liked hearing her mother use English expressions that she learned at work. "I guess so," was all she said this morning. She wished that getting up on the wrong side of bed was her only problem. She wished that she'd never even heard of Tom Connors.

Vatsana's mother gave Ketsy a ride to the place where she waited for the schoolbus. A few minutes later, Vatsana left her house and walked to Becky's house, the way she usually did. On the way to school, Becky talked a lot and Vatsana mostly listened, but Becky didn't seem to notice.

Vatsana couldn't concentrate on her schoolwork that morning. Even in Mrs. O'Malia's class, which she usually liked, she found it hard to pay attention and she was glad that Mrs. O'Malia didn't call on her. The one good thing about school that day was that Tom Connors didn't show up for either of the classes Vatsana had with him. Maybe he was playing hookey, Vatsana thought. She hoped the school would find out and that Tom would get in a lot of trouble.

When school was finally over that day, Vatsana was relieved. Becky was coming over to her house to help teach Ketsy more English. Maybe Becky and Ketsy could study English together without her, Vatsana thought. She just didn't feel like helping with an English lesson today. But she didn't feel like explaining why not either.

She and Becky walked home from school together and again Becky talked and Vatsana mostly listened. Vatsana didn't think that Becky noticed she was quieter than usual.

When they got to Becky's house, Becky stopped. "I want to show you something," she said to Vatsana. "It's up in my room. I just finished it yesterday."

Becky let them into her house—her mom was still at work—and they went upstairs to Becky's room. "Close your eyes," Becky said to Vatsana when they stood outside her room.

Vatsana closed her eyes and Becky led her into the room. "Okay now," Becky said. "You can open your eyes."

Becky had a big room, with a bed and bureau and armchair. Her desk was on one side of the room, by a row of windows which looked out on the backyard. An easel stood next to the desk and there was a painting propped up on it.

Vatsana stared at the picture. Their own faces—hers and Becky's—smiled back at her. The faces weren't quite the same as in real life but close enough. In the picture, she and Becky were standing close together, with their arms around each other.

"I used the picture my mom took of the two of us to help me," Becky explained.

There was a lump in Vatsana's throat, maybe because the picture was so nice. It gave her a warm feeling about her and Becky. They looked different from each other, of course. But they felt close—a lot closer than she and Ketsy did.

Becky smiled at Vatsana. "Do you like it?"

"It's really good," she managed to say. "I like it a lot." Then all of a sudden she started to cry.

"What's wrong Vatsana?" she heard Becky say. Vatsana tried to stop herself from crying but she couldn't. So she hid her face in her hands while her shoulders shook, and that same hurting feeling she'd had yesterday filled her chest.

"Tell me what's wrong, okay?" she heard Becky say. "Come on, Vatsana." She felt Becky put her arm around her, just like in the picture. That helped some, but it didn't stop her tears.

Finally she was all cried out. She wiped her eyes with the palms of her hands and blew her nose with the Kleenex Becky handed her. She looked at the patterned green rug on Becky's floor, then at the green and white bedspread that matched the rug. She felt embarrassed and it was easier to look somewhere else than to look at Becky.

When she finally met Becky's eyes, she saw that Becky didn't look embarrassed or scornful or anything like that. Instead she looked puzzled and concerned.

"Why were you crying?" Becky asked in a quieter than usual voice. She smiled a little. "I hope the picture wasn't that bad."

Vatsana hestitated. She still didn't want to talk about Tom Connors. She didn't even want to think about what happened with him. But Becky was her closest friend after all. Maybe she could just tell Becky and nobody else.

"The picture is beautful," Vatsana said. "It isn't that." Then she told Becky about running into Tom on the way home from school yesterday. About the way he had looked at her. And how he had called her chink and gook and said all those other things to her. Telling Becky made Vatsana feel angry all over again. And scared too. She still felt scared about the way Tom Connors had treated her.

"Tom Connors is a racist jerk," Becky said. She looked angrier than Vatsana had ever seen her. "People like him ought to keep to themselves and not bother anybody else with their stupid ideas."

Vatsana nodded. She liked the idea of Tom Connors staying away from other people. Especially of him staying far away from her. "I'm sorry I wasn't there yesterday," Becky said a moment later.

Vatsana was surprised to hear Becky say she was sorry. None of what happened was her fault. "He probably wouldn't have said all that stuff if you'd been there," she said. "He just would have waited for another time."

Becky still looked angry. She got up from the bed and paced around the room. "We can't let him get away with that kind of stuff."

"I don't want to either," Vatsana said quickly. "But what can we do?"

"You could tell one of the teachers. Like Mrs. O'Malia."

"But it didn't happen at school," Vatsana said. She hadn't told Becky about the way Tom Connors hassled her in Mr. Hansen's class. What Tom had said to her yesterday was bad enough. She didn't want Becky to know how many other times Tom had given her trouble. If Becky knew all that, maybe she'd figure that Vatsana was the kind of person who would let someone push her around and make her feel scared. And then maybe Becky wouldn't want to be friends with her anymore.

"I think you should decide what to do," Becky said, "because you're the one Tom is being jerky to. But I'll help you if there's anything I can do."

"Thanks," Vatsana said. "I'll think about what to do." She didn't have any ideas right now, and she didn't know what else to say.

By the time Vatsana got home from Becky's house, it was almost dinner time. She stared at her face in the bathroom mirror to see if it looked okay. She didn't want anyone in her family to know she'd been crying.

Ketsy didn't ask her why she and Becky hadn't been there for her usual English lesson. Vatsana was glad that Ketsy wasn't the type of person who always had to worm as much information out of you as possible. But she still wished that she and Ketsy weren't sharing a room so she would have a place to be alone.

"Ketsy is going to take dancing lessons," Vatsana's mother announced at dinner that evening. "She's going to study with Mrs. Songvilay." Ketsy smiled when Vatsana's mother said that, then looked down at the table. She looked embarrassed but happy.

"Ketsy studied dancing in Laos," Aunt Lavanny added, "so Mrs. Songvilay thinks that she will be an advanced student, and she can learn to do one of the special dances for the New Year."

Mrs. Songvilay taught Lao dancing to a few girls once a week. Vatsana's mother had tried to persuade her to learn, but Vatsana hadn't wanted to. It was bad enough, she figured, that she had to go to Lao language class one evening a week. Anyway, she didn't think she'd be any good at dancing.

Vatsana's father looked at Ketsy with a smile. "We'll be glad to see you dance at the

New Year." That was in the middle of April, and there was always a big celebration.

Even Vyvone, who mostly seemed preoccupied with schoolwork these days, thought Ketsy's dancing was a good idea. "That'll be great," he said to Ketsy. "I'll be there watching you for sure."

"Me too," Souk echoed, grinning at Ketsy.

Ketsy smiled back at all of them. Vatsana was the only one who wasn't smiling. She didn't see why Ketsy's dancing was such a big deal.

After dinner, Vatsana and Ketsy both went upstairs. Vatsana sat at her desk to do homework and Ketsy sat on her bed and started reading her English book from school.

Vatsana opened her science book, but it was hard to concentrate. She was still upset about Tom Connors, although talking with Becky had helped a lot. She felt kind of weird about Ketsy too. Maybe it was because Ketsy was good at something like dancing. It wasn't as if Vatsana wanted to study Lao dancing herself. But she wished that she really were the graceful type the way David Stafford had said.

Probably dancing lessons helped make you more graceful. Maybe that was why Ketsy liked them. But Vatsana still didn't see why Ketsy would want to study Lao dancing now that she was living in the United States.

"Why don't you learn to do American dancing?" Vatsana asked Ketsy.

Ketsy looked up from her book. She had a surprised expression on her face. "Maybe I can learn to do American dancing too," she said in Lao. "I would like that."

"You're living in America now," Vatsana continued. "American people don't care about Lao dancing. They like American dancing."

Ketsy looked confused. "I don't understand very much about America yet. Sometimes I feel like a baby again, there's so much for me to learn."

Vatsana waited. She wasn't sure what Ketsy was trying to say. "I know Laos isn't my home anymore," Ketsy said slowly. "I'm glad my mother and I could come to the United States. But I miss Laos sometimes. So when I do the Lao dancing, it makes me feel better inside."

Vatsana looked at Ketsy. Ketsy was wearing American clothes now, jeans and a sweater. She looked as American as Vatsana did. But Ketsy talks like my mother and father do, Vatsana thought. All of them think stuff about Laos is so important.

Maybe that wasn't Ketsy's fault, but it all kind of irritated Vatsana. She didn't know if she could ever feel like a sister with a cousin who was so different.

12

The next morning on the way to school, Vatsana told Becky about Ketsy's dancing lessons.

Becky's reaction surprised Vatsana. "That's neat," she said. "A couple of years ago my mom talked me into taking a class in Israeli folk dancing," Becky added. "She said it would be a lot of fun plus a good way for me to learn something more about Jewish culture."

"Did you like that kind of dancing?" Vatsana asked.

"It was fun," Becky said. She grinned at Vatsana. "Much as I hate to admit it, I think my mom was right. You know, I've never felt bad about being Jewish. But if you're Jewish you're always a little bit different. You don't get a tree at Christmas or Christmas presents like other kids. Maybe that's why it was kind of neat to learn about Israeli dancing."

While Mrs. Peterson was marking the attendance in her health class, Vatsana thought about what Becky had said. It kind of made sense, she could see that. She didn't understand why Becky felt different though. So what if she was Jewish. Becky's mother and father and grandparents were all Americans. Becky's mom didn't speak a foreign language at home the way Vatsana's mother and father did.

At the beginning of class, Mrs. O'Malia asked Becky, Vatsana, David Stafford, and a boy named Richard Allen to come up to her desk. "The compositions all four of you wrote on special events are very good," Mrs. O'Malia told them in a quiet voice. "I'd like you to read them to the class if that's okay with you."

"Sure," Becky said. David and Richard said it was fine with them too.

Vatsana looked at the floor. She didn't really want to read her composition to the class. But she felt bad saying "no" to Mrs. O'Malia. Especially after Becky, David, and Richard had all agreed.

"Is that okay with you, Vatsana?" Mrs. O'Malia asked. "If you'd rather not read your composition, that's fine."

"It's okay. I'll read it." Vatsana said quickly. Her stomach clenched a little when she said that. She'd read a composition in class once before, and nobody had laughed at her or anything while she was reading it. But her last composition had been about Egypt, which they were all studying then. Vatsana figured that no one in her class had even heard of a *baci* ceremony before.

Mrs. O'Malia smiled at her. "Your composition is an interesting one. I'm sure the class will enjoy hearing it."

They went over their homework for a few minutes. Then Mrs. O'Malia returned their compositions on special events. After that she said that the four of them would read their papers.

Becky read her composition about a bat mitzvah first. Vatsana admired the way Becky read in such a strong, clear voice. Becky was lucky not to be shy.

After Becky was finished, and a few kids had made some comments, David and Richard read their papers. David's was about Christmas and Richard's about Halloween.

It was Vatsana's turn next. She started to read in a quiet voice, then made herself talk louder. She could feel her palms get sweaty and her stomach tense as she read. She tried not to look at any of the other kids or worry about what they were thinking.

The class was quiet for a minute after Vatsana finished reading. Then David Stafford raised his hand. "That was neat to hear about. I like the part where everybody ties strings and makes wishes."

"I liked that part too," Becky said. "Plus the decoration thing with fruit and flowers and candles sounded pretty."

Vatsana sat looking down at her desk. She was waiting for some other kids to raise their hands and say that the *baci* ceremony was strange or weird. But nobody said anything like that.

It was a lucky thing that Tom Connors wasn't in class today, Vatsana thought. He would have said something mean to her about her composition, either in the class or later. So she was really glad that Tom was sick or something. She hoped he'd stay that way for a few more days.

Becky and Vatsana ate lunch together as usual. "I liked your composition," Vatsana told Becky.

"Thanks," Becky said. She ate a forkful of the tuna casserole they'd both gotten for lunch, made a face, then turned to face Vatsana. "I liked yours too. The *baci* ceremony sounded really interesting. I wish I could see one sometime."

"Maybe the next time my family has one you could come," Vatsana said quickly. She still felt guilty about not inviting Becky sooner to the *baci* ceremony for Aunt Lavanny and Ketsy.

"That'd be great," Becky said enthusiastically. She finished her glass of milk. "Meanwhile, I've got a great idea."

"About Tom Connors?"

Becky looked serious for a moment. "You're right. We have to find some way of dealing with that jerk. But this is a better idea than that." She smiled mysteriously. "You've got two guesses."

Vatsana's mind was blank. "I give up," she finally said.

Becky ate more of her casserole. "Well, okay. I'll let you off the hook. Last night I remembered you said you'd never been skiing. I think David Stafford was right. That is un-Oregonian." Becky had a pleased expression on her face. "So I asked my mom if she would take you and me and Ketsy cross-country skiing sometime soon and she said that she would this weekend."

"I don't have skis or anything," Vatsana said.

"That's okay. We can rent all that stuff. And I can loan you and Ketsy some things."

"It sounds neat," Vatsana said. Spending the day with Becky and her mom would be fun.

"Is skiing hard to learn?" she asked Becky a minute later. She hoped you didn't have to be "the graceful type" to go skiing.

Becky laughed. "Cross-country skiing is a lot like walking. Anybody can do it."

Vatsana had to smile. "I guess anybody includes me."

"I bet Ketsy will be good at skiing," Becky said. "Dancing must give her good balance."

Vatsana nodded. Ketsy would probably be a lot better than she would. It was a selfish thought, but part of her wished that Ketsy didn't have to go too.

"So do you think you can come?" Becky asked.

"Probably," Vatsana said. "I'll have to talk to my mother and father and Aunt Lavanny."

"Tell them that my mom is a good skier. And that she'll take us all on an easy trail."

"I'll tell them that," Vatsana promised. "I'm pretty sure they'll say okay."

13

Saturday was clear and sunny. Even though the air got cooler as they headed toward the mountain, the sunshine made the day feel warm.

"It looks as if it's going to be an ideal day for skiing," Becky's mom said. She had short brown hair which curled around her face and a warm smile like Becky's. Vatsana liked her a lot.

"Yeah, we're pretty lucky," Becky said. She grinned at Vatsana and Ketsy.

As they drove up toward Government Camp, they could see the snow-covered summit of Mount Hood above them. "Mountain is beautiful," Ketsy said in her slow English.

"It sure is," Vatsana agreed. She'd been up to Mount Hood before, although not nearly as much as Becky had, but it still gave her a chill down her spine to see the mountain looming above them like that.

Because it was later in the season, they had to go higher up to find a place that had enough snow to ski on. "There's a good place a little further up," Becky's mom said. "It's really a road, but when it's covered with snow, it's a good place to ski."

When they got to the right spot, Becky's mom parked the car in the snowplowed area by the side of the road. It was even sunnier up here than it was in Portland and the sunshine reflecting off the snowbank was blindingly bright. Vatsana was glad Becky had warned her and Ketsy that they needed to bring sunglasses.

"The snow is so beautiful," Ketsy said in Lao. Her eyes were sparkling, and she had an excited smile on her face.

"I guess you've never seen snow before, huh?" Becky said.

When Vatsana translated that, Ketsy shook her head. She bent down and touched a snowbank. "I think snow is very cold," she added.

That was a dumb thing to say, Vatsana thought. She felt stupid translating it into English. Everybody knew that snow was cold. She hoped that Ketsy wasn't going to talk like that all day.

Becky helped Vatsana and Ketsy with their skis. Once her skis were on, Vatsana didn't know what to do. It felt funny having these two long skinny things attached to her boots. Becky looked at the way Vatsana was standing and started laughing. That made Vatsana laugh too instead of worrying about what to do next.

Becky and her mom showed Vatsana and Ketsy how to move in cross country skis. The trail was almost level where it started out, so pretty soon both Vatsana and Ketsy were skiing along it.

Skiing was kind of fun, Vatsana decided. But it was hard work too. She envied the way Becky and her mom glided smoothly along the trail. They didn't have to watch their feet all the time and their skis didn't cross in front of them. Still, Vatsana hadn't fallen down yet, so she figured she was doing okay.

It was so beautiful up here anyway that Vatsana was glad they had come. A layer of snow covered each branch on the evergreen trees. They passed a stream with cornices of snow overhanging the banks, and then a place where the snow piled up alongside the trail in tall drifts. The bright sunshine made the snow glisten as if someone had scattered pieces of glitter in it.

All of it made Vatsana happy. Even if she wasn't the most graceful skier in the world, she was glad to be up here on the mountain, and especially glad that she and Becky were friends.

The trail climbed for a while, but slowly and gently. When they came to a flat, sunny place surrounded by fir trees, Becky's mom said that she was hungry and that it was time to stop for lunch.

Becky's mom had given them each a square of foam rubber to put in their backpacks. Now they took out the pieces of foam, which were just big enough to sit on.

"All right," Becky's mom said. "Who wants turkey and cheese sandwiches and who wants salami?"

Becky groaned. "I thought you weren't going to bring salami this time." She made a face at Vatsana. "That's why my mom and dad got divorced. He hated my mom's salami sandwiches."

Becky's mom laughed and threw some snow at Becky. "Just for that," she said, "you'll have to eat all the salami."

Becky groaned again. "Oh no. A fate worse than death."

Becky's mom pretended to relent. "Well okay," she said. "You can have turkey and cheese after all."

She handed turkey and cheese sandwiches to Vatsana and Ketsy too. "Don't worry. I know I'm the only one who likes salami."

Vatsana translated for Ketsy some of what Becky and her mom were saying, but Ketsy still looked puzzled. Vatsana bit into her sandwich, which tasted great. It figured that Ketsy was confused, Vatsana realized. In Laos, people hardly ever got divorced. So how was Ketsy supposed to understand how Becky and her mom could joke about her mom's divorce?

Becky's mom opened up a big thermos and poured them all cups of hot chocolate. They sat finishing their sandwiches and drinking hot chocolate.

"I'm glad we're not at school right now," Vatsana said. She didn't think they could possibly meet Tom Connors anywhere on the mountain.

"Yeah," Becky said. "Even the food is better here."

Becky's mother laughed. "You two sound like future drop outs."

Vatsana translated all that for Ketsy, but Ketsy didn't understand that they were joking. "Why do you want to leave school?" Ketsy asked in Lao.

"We don't really," Becky explained. "Sometimes school gets to us though."

Becky's mother sat there drinking her hot chocolate and listening to them. There was a smile on her face as if she were laughing at what they were saying but not really at them.

Vatsana wondered if Becky's mom would laugh if Vatsana told her about Tom Connors. That was a scary thought. But Becky's mom always seemed so nice. And she was a lot easier to talk to than Vatsana's own mother and father. She understood things a lot more.

"Sometimes I do want to leave school," Vatsana said all of a sudden.

"How come?" Becky's mother asked her. She didn't act like that was a funny thing to say.

Vatsana hesitated. She looked at Becky, but Becky didn't say anything.

"It's because of Tom Connors," Vatsana finally said. "He's in two of my classes and he keeps on bothering me."

After she said that much, Vatsana felt as if she couldn't stop herself from going on. She told Becky's mom about the things Tom Connors had said to her after school, and the time he'd called her chink and gook after Mr. Hansen's math class, and the way he'd been mean to her in other ways for a while before that. She told Becky's mom more than she'd even told Becky before today.

It was scary to say all that. Vatsana started to shake a little as she talked. But it felt good to talk too, in a strange kind of way. It felt as if all that stuff was like a river that had been dammed up inside her. And now the dam was gone and the river came pouring out of her.

Becky's mom didn't say anything until Vatsana was finished talking. "I'm glad you told us all that," she said then.

"I am too," Becky put in. "I knew Tom Connors was creepy, but I didn't know how bad he was."

Becky sounded angry, but at Tom Connors rather than at her, Vatsana thought. Neither Becky nor her mom were acting like it was Vatsana's fault for letting Tom Connors be that way with her.

Becky's mom poured them all a little more hot chocolate. "Prejudice is a strange thing," she said a moment later. "When we're prejudiced we don't like someone just because they're Asian or black or Jewish or whatever. Prejudice blinds some people to who other people really are." She took a sip of her hot chocolate. "It sounds as if Tom Connors hardly knows you, Vatsana, but he doesn't like you just because you're Asian."

Vatsana nodded. That was right, she thought.

"Prejudice can hurt," Becky's mom continued. "My mother once told me about when she was a girl and some kids called her dirty Jew. She cried a lot afterwards, she told me that too."

"My mother told her mother what had happened. That was your great grandmother Esther," Becky's mom said to Becky.

"My Grandma Esther told my mother to forget about the boys. She said that they showed how stupid they were by the names they called her. But the important thing was for my mother to understand that no matter what the boys said, she was really a good person."

Becky's mom looked right at Vatsana. "You're a good person too. Becky tells me what good friends the two of you are."

Vatsana swallowed hard. What Becky's mom said made her feel warm inside.

"I know that Vatsana's a good person," Becky said a minute later. "But she can't just forget about Tom Connors."

"I know she can't," Becky's mom agreed. "But it's important for Vatsana to know that Tom Connors doesn't see what she's really like."

They were all getting cold by then, so they packed up their garbage from lunch and headed back toward the car. Since it was Vatsana and Ketsy's first skiing trip, Becky's mom decided they should turn back now before Vatsana and Ketsy got too tired.

As they skied back down the trail, Vatsana thought about what Becky's mom had said. Becky's mom didn't think it was her fault at all that Tom Connors said all that stuff to her. It was his fault for being prejudiced. She was an okay person even if Tom Connors acted like a creep.

She had to do something about Tom Connors. Becky was right about that. And she still didn't know what she could do to make Tom stop bothering her. But she felt a lot better inside herself now.

She did fall a few times when the trail sloped more sharply, but the snow was soft so falling didn't hurt. Becky showed her how to lay her skis together and push herself back up. "Everybody falls down when they're learning," Becky said. "I sure did."

Vatsana was glad to hear that. If she could learn to ski, maybe some part of her was "the graceful type" after all.

Ketsy had been skiing ahead of Vatsana, between Becky and Becky's mom. When they got back to the car and took off their skis, Ketsy walked over to Vatsana.

"I'm glad we went skiing today," Ketsy said to Vatsana in Lao. "I'm glad you and your friend Becky invited me."

Ketsy had been okay, Vatsana decided. She hadn't tried to talk about Laos all the time or anything like that.

"No problem," Vatsana said to Ketsy in English. She and Becky had explained what that meant to Ketsy, so she figured that Ketsy would understand.

Tom Connors was back in school the next Monday. Vatsana heard him telling another boy that his father had taken him on a fishing trip. Tom had a sullen look on his face. So maybe it hadn't been that good a trip. Vatsana hoped that Tom hadn't caught any fish.

"Did you miss me?" Tom said to her later, as she took her seat in Mr. Hansen's class.

Vatsana wasn't going to say anything, but all of a sudden that made her mad. "I wouldn't miss anybody who kept calling me dumb names." It was kind of scary saying that, but it felt good too.

For a moment Tom looked surprised. Maybe because Vatsana didn't usually answer him back. Then his mouth drew together into tight, angry lines. "Watch out, chink," he said in a low voice. "My friends and I have got plans for you."

All the rest of Mr. Hansen's class, Vatsana had a knotted-up feeling in the pit of her stomach. She wasn't sorry she'd talked back to Tom, and she knew Becky and her mom wouldn't be either. But she worried about what Tom and his friends were going to do.

"See you later, chink," Tom Connors said to her in the hall afterward. He had a half smile on his face, but it was such a mean-looking smile it gave her chills along her spine.

Tom kept on hassling her day after day. He called her names, mostly outside of class so the teachers wouldn't hear. One time Vatsana saw Tom in the hallway, talking to Joe Rinella and Dan Johnson, a couple of boys Tom hung out with. As Vatsana passed them, Joe whistled at her.

"Nice looking chinkee," Tom said. Joe and Dan smirked.

Vatsana turned her head away and pretended not to care what they said. But as she walked down the hall, she felt their eyes still following her.

Every time Tom bothered her, it gave her a weird feeling. But she tried to remember what Becky's mom had said—that she was a good person no matter what Tom thought. Once in a while she said something back to Tom. Mostly she tried to ignore him. She figured she could do that as long as Tom and his friends didn't bother her any worse than now.

Meanwhile it rained. Almost every day when Vatsana woke up in the morning, she could hear the patter of rain coming down. Outside, the sky turned a chalky color, or sometimes a mottled gray.

As she did every spring, Vatsana got used to walking to school in the rain, watching for puddles so her shoes wouldn't get totally soaked. It was a much gentler rain than the monsoons in Laos, Vatsana's mother said. In Laos, everyone was glad when the monsoons came because they helped bring a good rice harvest. Here in Oregon, Vatsana watched the grass turn greener and the trees grow their first pale green spring leaves.

When Vatsana and Becky walked to school together, they wore the hoods of their raincoats up to keep their hair dry. That meant they had to walk closer together so they could talk.

"Is Tom Connors still bugging you?" Becky asked Vatsana one morning.

Vatsana nodded. "He still says some dumb stuff. But I think about what your mom said, that it just shows how stupid he is."

"I wish we could do more about that jerk," Becky said.

"So do I," Vatsana agreed. But she still couldn't think what she and Becky could do.

In Mrs. O'Malia's class, they were studying the Renaissance now. But one day Mrs. O'Malia had them take a break from that. "I want you to write another composition today," she told the class. She waited until the usual groans subsided. "Pick a person that you know and tell me as much as you can about what that person is like."

Becky was Vatsana's closest friend, but it felt kind of weird to write about her. She liked Becky's mom a lot, but probably she didn't know enough about her. Vatsana considered writing about her younger brother Souk. Then she changed her mind and decided to write about Ketsy.

She started with how her Aunt Lavanny and Ketsy had come to Portland a couple of months ago. At first Ketsy was shy, Vatsana said. But now she's easier to talk with. She's learning English at school, so that helps a lot.

Vatsana stopped writing for a moment. What else could she say about Ketsy? My mother says that Ketsy and I will be like sisters, Vatsana went on. But I don't think my mother is right. Ketsy and I look a lot the same. But Ketsy thinks like someone from Laos and I think like an American. Even though Ketsy is a good person, it's hard for me to feel close with her because we think so differently.

Vatsana wrote more about Ketsy so that Mrs. O'Malia would understand how different Ketsy was. After a while Mrs. O'Malia said it was almost time for them to stop writing. Vatsana read over her paper. Then she handed it in with all the others.

When Mrs. O'Malia gave back their compositions a couple of days later, she wrote at the bottom of Vatsana's composition that she enjoyed it very much. She also wrote a note saying that she'd like Vatsana to talk to her after class today.

Vatsana went up to Mrs. O'Malia's desk when their class was over. She was surprised to see that Becky, David Stafford, and Richard Allen were waiting to talk to Mrs. O'Malia too. She hoped that Mrs. O'Malia didn't want the four of them to read their compositions to the class again.

"All of you have been doing excellent writing this year," Mrs. O'Malia said to them. "So I thought you might be interested in a special project—a little magazine with the best writing from our class in it."

"Would the four of you be willing to help with that? It would take some time after school for a few days," Mrs. O'Malia explained.

"I think it's a great idea," Becky volunteered. Vatsana, Richard, and David all said they'd be glad to help.

Mrs. O'Malia smiled at them. "Okay," she said. "We'll start tomorrow after school. We'll all meet here at two-thirty."

When they went to Mrs. O'Malia's room after school the next day, she handed each of them a pile of papers. "Read through them and pick out the ones you think are interesting and well written," she told them.

Vatsana chose a desk near a window and got to work. She found several papers that she thought were especially good. Some were stories, true or made up ones, and others were compositions about different subjects.

When Vatsana saw that the next paper in her pile was by Tom Connors, she covered it up with a book. She rested her hands on the book as if their weight would make Tom's paper disappear. She didn't want to read anything Tom had written. Even if Tom's paper was good, she didn't want it in their magazine. Maybe she should hide his paper in the book and throw it out when no one was looking.

She knew Mrs. O'Malia would be really mad, though, if she found out Vatsana had done that. Anyway, she was a little bit curious about what Tom would say in his paper. So after a minute she started to read it.

Tom's paper turned out to be a story about a boy whose father lost his leg in the Vietnam war. The story wasn't very well written, and Vatsana was about to add it to the pile of rejects. Then she changed her mind and read it again.

Vatsana folded over a corner of Tom's paper and then smoothed it out again. Tom's story didn't deserve to be put in the pile for good papers. But it was interesting, and Vatsana wasn't sorry that she'd read it after all.

She wondered if Tom Connors's father really had lost his leg in the Vietnam War. Maybe that was why Tom hated Asians so much.

All that didn't make him any less of a creep, she thought. It didn't give him any right to call her names. But if she understood Tom better, maybe she could figure out something that would make him leave her alone.

After school the next day, Vatsana, Becky, David, and Richard went to Mrs. O'Malia's room again. The piles of papers to be read for the first time were smaller today.

They each took some papers and sat reading them. After a few minutes, David came over to where Vatsana was sitting. "Hey," he said to her. "I like your composition about Ketsy. She sounds like a neat person."

"Thanks," Vatsana said. She felt kind of embarrassed but good at the same time.

By the time their magazine editing group was ready to leave that afternoon, they had finished reading all the papers for the first time. "We're working well together," Mrs. O'Malia told them. "Tomorrow we'll make our final decisions about which papers we want in our magazine."

Richard Allen went home in a different direction. But David walked a few blocks with Becky and Vatsana before he turned down his own street. "See you tomorrow, fellow editors," he said to them as he left.

"That David is sure nice," Becky said as soon as they had gotten far enough away from him. "I wish a lot more of the boys in our class were like him."

"Me too," Vatsana agreed. Their health teacher had told them one time that boys matured more slowly than girls. Judging by a lot of the other boys in their class, Vatsana could see that that was true.

Even though they got out of school later than usual, Becky still went over to Vatsana's house that day. They would have helped Ketsy with her English, but she started telling them about the dance she was learning to do for the Lao New Year.

"This dance is part of our tradition," Ketsy said in Lao. "In the villages the people fill a big jar with rice wine for celebrations. So at the New Year we dance around that kind of jar and pretend to drink the wine."

Ketsy showed them a little bit of the dance. While she danced, she slowly turned her hands but kept her fingers bent back in a gracefully curved position.

"That's great," Becky said. "I wish I could dance like that. It looks hard to do."

"I can show you," Ketsy said eagerly.

Becky laughed. "Go ahead, but I know I'm not going to look the way you do when you dance."

Becky stood up and let Ketsy start teaching her how to stand and how to hold her hands. Vatsana watched the two of them together. Becky didn't look at all the way Ketsy did when she danced. But Becky didn't look as if that was bothering her either.

That was something she really liked about Becky, Vatsana thought. The way she'd try to do something without getting embarrassed or worried about how she was doing. She didn't seem to be afraid, the way Vatsana was sometimes, about people laughing at her or putting her down.

"I think that's enough of a lesson for today," Becky finally said. She grinned at both Vatsana and Ketsy. "Maybe I'll be ready to dance at the Lao New Year 10 years from now."

Ketsy smiled. "You teach me English. I teach you dance," she said in English.

Becky and Ketsy were smiling at each other but Vatsana just sat there. Great, she thought to herself. Maybe I can take tickets at the door or something.

Of course, it wasn't as if there was anything wrong about Becky's learning Lao dancing if that was what she really wanted to do. Sometimes, though, Vatsana wondered why Becky was more interested in learning about Lao stuff than she was.

16

In Mr. Hansen's class the next day, Tom Connors acted jerky as usual. When Mr. Hansen was busy on the other side of the room, Tom made a face at Vatsana, using his fingers to make his eyes look slanty and biting his lower lip as if he had buck teeth. His face looked really ugly that way. Vatsana wondered if Tom thought all Asian people looked like the stupid face he was making.

"Bye-bye, chinko," Tom said to Vatsana outside the class.

"Bye-bye, dumbo," Vatsana retorted. She had to say something back to Tom once in a while. Even if he kept on acting like a creep to her. That way she felt better about herself anyway.

After school, Vatsana, Becky, David, Richard, and Mrs. O'Malia read through the pile of good papers they had set aside. Vatsana's composition about Ketsy was in that pile, and all of them liked it. "We'll definitely put that into the magazine," Mrs. O'Malia said.

Vatsana felt proud when Mrs. O'Malia said that, and a little scared too. She wondered how the other kids in her class would like her story. And if Tom Connors read it, what would he do?

Well, she'd find out, Vatsana figured. Maybe there'd be more trouble between her and Tom. Maybe he and his friends would try to do something bad to her. But she was still glad her composition was going to be in the magazine.

She didn't tell anybody in her family about that. She'd wait to show them when the magazine came out, Vatsana decided. At dinner that night, Vatsana listened to her father, mother, and aunt talk about plans for the Lao New Year. The celebration was only a week and a half away now.

Vyvone grinned at their father. "We're looking forward to hearing your speech."

Vatsana's father smiled. "I hope I can give some good thoughts for the New Year."

Vatsana's father was a member of the Lao Association, which was organizing the celebration. It was an honor for him to speak at the New Year, Vatsana's mother had told her.

"Vyvone's got a date for the dance," Souk said with a grin.

Vyvone frowned at Souk but Aunt Lavanny looked surprised. In Laos, dating wasn't the custom, Vatsana knew.

Vatsana's father looked at Vyvone. "Lao ideas and American ideas are different. And I know we can't keep all the old customs here. Now Vyvone is 19 and a college student. He's old enough to decide many things for himself."

Vyvone had an embarrassed look on his face. Still, he was probably glad their father had said what he did, Vatsana guessed. She and Souk and Vyvone were lucky that their mother and father were willing to accept some American ideas. Not all Lao parents felt that way.

What if David Stafford asked her for a date, Vatsana suddenly imagined. That was a crazy idea. Hardly anybody in their seventh grade class was going out on dates. David was always friendly to her, but he was friendly to a lot of people.

Even if David did ask her, her parents would never let her go out with him. Vatsana knew that for sure. Their mother had told Vyvone that she didn't want him to date until he was finished with high school.

Vatsana helped her mother clear the table after dinner. Sometimes Vyvone did the dishes, but tonight he had to study for a test. So

Vatsana and Ketsy washed and dried the dishes while Vatsana's mother made lunches for them.

The dishes were almost done when Vatsana got an idea. "If Vyvone can bring a date to the New Year celebration, can I bring Becky?" she asked her mother.

Vatsana's mother smiled. "That's a good idea," she said in Lao.

"How about Becky and her mom both?" Vatsana added, in English, a moment later. She remembered how nice Becky's mom had been on the ski trip they'd taken.

"You should certainly invite Becky and her mother," Vatsana's mother said. "Tell them our whole family would like them to come. We'll get tickets for them and we'll all go together." She smiled at Vatsana again. "I'm glad you want to bring your friend to our Lao New Year."

Vatsana and Ketsy finished the dishes and went upstairs. "I hope Becky can come to the New Year," Ketsy said in Lao. "I'd like her to see the way my dance really looks."

Vatsana shrugged. "I'll ask Becky tomorrow." She did want Becky to come, but she wasn't inviting her for Ketsy's sake. Becky was still more her friend than Ketsy's friend, Vatsana figured.

On the way to school the next day, Vatsana asked Becky about coming to the Lao New Year.

"I'll ask my mom," Becky said. She sounded pretty enthusiastic about the idea.

The next few afternoons after school, Vatsana, Becky, Richard, and David met with Mrs. O'Malia and worked on the layout of the magazine. By the end of the week, they were finished, and Mrs. O'Malia said she would take the proofed pages to a copy place over the weekend. Next Monday, they would meet one more time to staple the pages together and then on Tuesday everybody in their class would get a copy of the paper.

They all felt excited when they left Mrs. O'Malia's room. David walked with them for a few blocks, and David and Becky were joking around with each other. "Maybe we'll win a Pulitzer Prize," Becky said.

"At least," David added.

Vatsana was quieter but she was excited too. Her story was going to be on the first page of the magazine. She was sure her parents would be pleased about that. Her father and mother wanted all of their children to do well in school. And even though her parents wanted her and her brothers to know how to speak Lao, they were glad to see them doing well in their English classes.

On Saturday Vatsana and Ketsy helped clean the house and do laundry. "The Lao New Year is next weekend," Vatsana's mother said, "so we have to start getting ready for it. In Laos," she reminded Vatsana, "everybody cleans their houses from top to bottom for the New Year. Then during the New Year we go to the temples and wash the statues of Buddha." She smiled at Ketsy. "You and your mother did that last year, didn't you?"

Ketsy nodded. "Yes, we did."

In her mother's eyes, Vatsana thought, Ketsy did everything right because she had grown up in Laos. That made Vatsana mad sometimes. Ketsy was supposed to go downtown with her and Becky this afternoon. In a way, it was too bad Ketsy wasn't going with Vatsana's mother and Aunt Lavanny to the Buddhist temple instead.

At least Vatsana's mother didn't make her and Ketsy go with her to the temple today. It wasn't the Lao New Year yet, but most people couldn't go to the temple in the middle of the week when it really started, so there was a ceremony today. Lots of people wouldn't go to it though. Vatsana's mother said that in the United States especially, the Lao New Year was more of a holiday for family and friends than an important religious holiday.

After Vatsana and Ketsy had lunch, Becky came over. It was cloudy that day but not raining—good weather for April in Portland. Vatsana, Becky, and Ketsy walked a few blocks to the bus stop and waited there until their bus came.

When they got on the bus, Becky found a seat first and Ketsy sat next to her. Going downtown with Ketsy had been Becky's idea. Vatsana sat right in front of them, so she could turn around and translate for Ketsy if she needed to.

"Are you excited about dancing at the New Year?" Becky asked Ketsy.

Ketsy smiled. "I am happy to dance at New Year," she said slowly.

Vatsana looked out the window. She was tired of hearing about Ketsy's dancing. She watched as the bus pulled up to a bus shelter and several more people got on.

Becky tapped Vatsana on the shoulder. "I want to tell Ketsy that you and I are helping with the writing magazine in Mrs. O'Malia's class."

Vatsana translated that for Ketsy and explained to her what kind of things would be in the magazine and what she and Becky were doing with it. As she said all that to Ketsy, she noticed that an older woman sitting right across the aisle from the three of them was staring at her.

It was probably because she was speaking Lao, Vatsana figured. Maybe the woman thought both she and Ketsy were refugees who'd only been here a short time.

Vatsana tried to forget about the woman. The bus was crossing the bridge over the Willamette River. She could see the river below—dark green and rippled by the wind. Across the river stood the tall buildings of downtown Portland.

Becky tapped Vatsana on the shoulder again. "Tell Ketsy that we're going to show her all the sights of downtown, all the weird people and everything."

Vatsana didn't say anything right away. She saw that the older woman across the aisle was watching the three of them again. She had a disapproving look on her face. Maybe the woman thought the way Tom Connors did— that refugees from Asia shouldn't have come to this country.

Becky was grinning at Vatsana, but all of a sudden Vatsana felt angry. She was tired of translating stuff for Ketsy. She didn't like people staring at her or thinking she wasn't American just because she was speaking a foreign language.

"Why don't you tell her that yourself?" Vatsana snapped. "Ketsy needs to speak English instead of Lao all the time."

Becky's expression changed from surprised to mad. "Forget it," she said in a sharp voice. "I don't need your help." She turned away from Vatsana and started talking to Ketsy.

When the bus came to their stop, Becky and Ketsy got off together and Vatsana followed them. She was already sorry about what she'd said. Ketsy's English still wasn't very good and Becky couldn't speak Lao. They really did need her to translate for them.

She would have said all that to Becky—and said that she was sorry too—but Becky wasn't paying any attention to her. She was still talking to Ketsy in very slow, simple English.

Vatsana felt as if she was tagging along while Becky showed Ketsy Pioneer Square. The square was a whole city block paved with red bricks. Brick steps led down to it and on one end there was a fountain made from brightly colored tiles.

Usually Vatsana liked watching all the different kinds of clothes and hairstyles on the people who hung around the square. Today she couldn't help noticing a boy whose hair was dyed green. Did Ketsy see him? she wondered. But right now she didn't really care about who was in the square or what Ketsy thought. Mostly Vatsana felt bad about her and Becky. Becky hadn't ever seemed as mad at her before.

After Pioneer Square, they walked up to the library as they had planned. The library was a three-story stone and brick building with trees around it and tall arched windows. It was one of Vatsana's favorite places downtown, but today she didn't enjoy being there the way she usually did. She got a lonely feeling as she watched Becky and Ketsy walking together.

At least Becky was speaking to her again though. Becky still looked kind of mad, but she did turn around to ask Vatsana'a advice about which of the easy-reading children's books Ketsy might like.

When they left the library, Becky decided they should take Ketsy to see the statue of Portlandia. "We've got enough time," Becky said. Vatsana just nodded. She wasn't going to argue with Becky any more today.

When they got to the statue, they stood on the far edge of the sidewalk and looked up at it. The statue was big enough to seem like a giant. A woman with strong arms and a peaceful expression on her face was holding what always reminded Vatsana of a pitchfork.

"It used to look like gold," Becky explained. She pointed to her ring to be sure Ketsy understood what gold was. "Now the color is changing to brown."

"How do you like the statue?" Vatsana asked Ketsy in Lao. Maybe if she spoke Lao to Ketsy, Becky would understand that she was sorry for what she said earlier.

"It's beautiful," Ketsy answered in Lao. "It's so big and peaceful that it reminds me of a statue of Buddha in a temple in Vientiane. I used to like to go to that temple and bring flowers to the Buddha. Portlandia is a lot different, but their faces are a little bit the same."

Vatsana translated that for Becky. "That's neat," Becky said. She didn't look mad anymore. "We can think of Portlandia as the Buddha of Portland."

Vatsana thought that was a strange thing to say. Buddha and Portlandia weren't really the same at all. But Ketsy laughed when Vatsana translated what Becky said. It was getting later by now. They walked back to the mall and waited with the crowds of Saturday shoppers until their bus came.

This time Vatsana and Ketsy sat on a seat together. Vatsana let Ketsy have the window seat so she could see more of Portland. Becky sat right behind them and she tapped Vatsana's arm to get her to turn around in her seat.

"I bet Ketsy learned a lot about Portland today," Becky said. She smiled at Vatsana, but her smile looked a little uncertain.

Probably Becky was sorry they'd been mad at each other, Vatsana thought. "I think Ketsy had a good time," she said to Becky. Becky didn't say anything more and Vatsana didn't either. But Vatsana knew that they were friends again.

The bus crossed the bridge and headed east. It would take the bus a while to get to their street with all the people getting off at each stop. Vatsana liked long bus rides, partly because she could let her mind wander. Right now she was thinking about how Portlandia reminded Ketsy of the statue of Buddha in a temple in Vientiane. Vatsana tried to picture Ketsy going to the temple, bringing flowers to the statue of Buddha. All that seemed so far away. So different from life in Portland.

Becky didn't seem to care about Ketsy being different. Even if old ladies stared at them on the bus, Becky still wanted to be friends with Ketsy.

Maybe Becky had the right idea, Vatsana decided. Probably people like the old lady on the bus were the ones who were wrong.

Ketsy was a nice person after all. She'd learned a lot about the United States already, even though she'd only been here a short time. So maybe it didn't matter very much if Ketsy was still more foreign than American.

17

On Monday after school, Vatsana, Becky, Richard, and David helped Mrs. O'Malia collate and staple copies of the magazine for their English class. "We've done a good job," Mrs. O'Malia said when they were finished. She looked happy. "Tomorrow I'll pass out the magazines in class."

The kids were sure to read her story since it was on the first page, Vatsana thought. That made her feel excited but nervous too.

Tuesday morning, after Mrs. O'Malia explained their next homework assignment, she handed out copies of the magazine to their class. "Many of you will see your own writing," Mrs. O'Malia said. "And this will give all of you a chance to read stories written by students in your own class."

Mrs. O'Malia gave them the rest of the time—about half the period—to read. Vatsana tried to concentrate, but it wasn't easy. The palms of her hands got sweaty as she wondered who was reading her story right now.

After class some kids came up to Vatsana. "Good story," Laura Chin said to Vatsana. "I liked it too," Marcia Watson said. "Maybe we can meet Ketsy sometime."

Vatsana couldn't help smiling. It was a real relief that the other kids liked her story about Ketsy. She was glad also that Marcia Watson wanted to meet Ketsy. One of these days Ketsy would be coming here to school, and Vatsana hoped that kids would be nice to her.

"Great magazine, huh?" Becky said excitedly to Vatsana as they walked toward the cafeteria.

"You bet it is," David said as he fell into step beside them. "I bet that's the best magazine a seventh grade class put out in a long time."

It was nice that day, so they decided to eat their lunches quickly and go outside. David went to play soccer with some other boys, but Vatsana and Becky walked across the schoolyard together. They were standing by the edge of the schoolyard, leaning against the fence, when Vatsana saw Tom Connors coming toward them. He was with his friends Joe Rinella and Dan Johnson.

"Uh oh," Becky said. "Here comes trouble."

Vatsana grimaced. "Yeah," she said. She saw that aside from Tom, Joe, and Dan, no other kids were close to her and Becky.

Tom came right up to Vatsana and stood there scowling at her. He was wearing dirty jeans and a black sweatshirt with a picture of a motorcycle on the front. Joe and Dan were on either side of him. They were standing shoulder to shoulder. Even though Joe and Dan weren't as tall as Tom, Vatsana couldn't see past them to the rest of the schoolyard. She didn't think anybody else could see her and Becky either.

"Hey, get out of our face," Becky said. She sounded defiant but a little uncertain too.

Tom and the other two boys didn't pay any attention to Becky. The three boys moved closer to Vatsana and Becky. Tom kicked gravel toward them and Joe and Dan snickered. When Becky tried to push Joe Rinella further away from her, he shoved her toward the fence. Tom and Dan both took another step forward so the three boys made a half circle around Becky and Vatsana.

The chain link fence pressed against Vatsana's back. She was glad that Becky was with her, but she still had a knot of fear in her stomach. What did Tom want with her now? What were he, Joe, and Dan going to do?

"I read your thing," Tom said sarcastically. He underlined "thing" with his voice.

"Good, wasn't it?" Becky put in.

Tom ignored Becky. He stared into Vatsana's eyes as if he were trying to force her to look at him. "I bet you and your gook family are really glad you brought some more gooks over to this country." Tom raised his voice. "That's another couple of gooks to go on welfare and take money from Americans."

"That's crazy," Becky blurted out.

Joe shoved Becky again, but Tom barely glanced at her. "I want to know what your gook friend has to say." He looked back at Vatsana. His voice was sarcastic. "Maybe you've been talking so much gook talk that you forgot how to speak English." He grinned at Joe and Dan. "No speekee English," he said in a phoney high voice.

Tom stabbed a finger at Vatsana's face— near her eyes. "See the slant eyes," he chanted.

Vatsana shoved Tom's hand away. Her stomach clenched. She was still afraid, but she was angry now too, angry enough that she didn't even hear what Becky was starting to say.

Vatsana looked straight at Tom Connors, staring at his red hair and the freckles that covered his pale skin. She felt herself start to shake but she made her voice stay steady. "I'm glad my aunt Lavanny and cousin Ketsy came here. They're not slant eyes or gooks. They're not on welfare either. Aunt Lavanny is going to get a job sewing as soon as her English is better."

Vatsana took a breath. "Aunt Lavanny and Ketsy are just as good as anybody else. They're a lot better people than you are," she said to Tom. "They don't go around calling other people names all the time."

"That's right," Becky added.

Tom Connors interrupted her. "She's just a gook, isn't she?" he said to Joe and Dan. "Little gookee girly come to U.S.A.," Tom said in a sing-song voice.

Tom's eyes narrowed. He leaned forward and spat on the ground near Vatsana's feet. He and Joe and Dan made their hands into fists. Vatsana could feel the hate coming from them, but most of all from Tom Connors. It felt almost as if he were hitting her.

Vatsana hunched over for a moment, staring at the blob of spit on the ground. "That's gross," she dimly heard Becky say. Vatsana looked back at Tom. She was so mad at him that she didn't feel at all afraid any more.

"You call all Asian people chinks and gooks," she said to Tom. "My mother and father came to the United States from Laos. But they're not bad people like you say they are."

Vatsana straightened her back so she was standing as tall as she could. She looked right into Tom's eyes. "I was born in the United States just like you were. I'm glad that I'm an American. But I'm part Lao too. And that's okay with me."

Tom screwed his mouth up as if he were going to spit again. "Go back to your own country."

This time Becky interrupted Tom. "That's a stupid way to think! Almost everybody's family came here from a different country. Just like my great grandparents who came from Russia."

Tom pointed at Becky. "I guess you like gooks real well then."

All of a sudden Vatsana had something else she wanted to say to Tom. "I read your story about your father losing his leg in Vietnam. Did that really happen?"

Tom looked surprised. He didn't know she knew about that, Vatsana realized.

"It's true," Tom said after a few seconds. He still sounded mad but his voice was lower now. "He stepped on a mine one of you gooks put there."

Vatsana took a deep breath. "There's a lot you don't know. My father was in the war too. He was a pilot in the Laotian air force. But he didn't fight against the American army."

She paused for a moment, then went on. "My father isn't the one who made your father lose his leg." She raised her voice. "My father fought on the American side."

"Ooh Tom," Joe Rinella said. Dan had a smirk on his face.

Joe and Dan were watching Tom now, Vatsana noticed, as if they were waiting to see what he would do next. Tom's hands were balled into fists and his face was turning red. "So what," he muttered. But he didn't say anything more or even look right at Vatsana.

A moment later the bell rang. Tom, Joe, and Dan headed off together. Vatsana and Becky stood and watched them go.

"You were great!" Becky said to Vatsana. "You really told those guys off. Especially that jerk, Tom Connors."

Vatsana felt a smile spreading across her face. Becky was smiling back at her.

"I'm glad I said all that stuff to Tom," Vatsana said as they walked back to the school. She was still all wound up from talking to him. But she felt good inside.

Tom Connors didn't bother Vatsana at all in Mr. Hansen's class. And even if he had, Vatsana didn't think she would have cared. Maybe she wouldn't ever worry any more about what Tom Connors said. The more she thought about him, the more stupid he seemed.

Vatsana, David, and Becky went to Mrs. O'Malia's room after school one last time. "I enjoyed working with all of you," Mrs. O'Malia said. "We ended up with an excellent magazine."

"It was fun working on it," Becky said.

"Me too," David agreed. Richard nodded.

"It was great," Vatsana said. She met Mrs. O'Malia's eyes and smiled back at her.

Vatsana, Becky, and David started walking home together the way they'd done most of the time since they began staying later at school to work on the magazine. Probably they wouldn't do that so much after today, Vatsana thought. The other boys might tease David if he was always walking home with girls. But probably she and Becky and David would still talk together sometimes.

"Hey," Becky said to David, "you know what?"

David grinned at her. "What?"

"Vatsana and I are going to the Lao New Year this Saturday night. My mom is coming plus Vatsana's whole family. We're going to eat Lao food and see Vatsana's cousin do a special Lao dance."

"That sounds great," David said. "My mom and dad and sister and I went to the Vietnamese New Year celebration a couple of times with the Nguyens. It was really interesting."

He turned to Vatsana. "Can anyone come to that?"

Vatsana wasn't sure why David was asking. "Sure. Anyone can come. You just have to buy tickets at the door."

"I'll talk to my mom and dad and sister," David said. "I don't think they have plans for Saturday. Maybe we'll go to the Lao New Year too."

David said goodbye and then turned down his block. "I hope David and his family do come to the New Year," Becky said a moment later. "That'd be fun."

"I guess so," Vatsana said. She liked David a lot. So maybe it would be fun if he and his family came to the Lao New Year. It would be interesting to meet David's mother and father and sister. But she just wasn't sure what it would be like to have David Stafford at the Lao New Year celebration.

Vatsana's house had a holiday feeling about it this Saturday. Everything was sparkling clean and the kitchen smelled of curry and garlic and cilantro. Vatsana's mother and her aunt Lavanny had been busy cooking special holiday food.

Vatsana's mother and Aunt Lavanny took scented water and washed the picture of Buddha and the little stone statue of Buddha that Aunt Lavanny had brought. Then Vatsana, Ketsy, and Souk did the same thing. "That brings good luck to you," Vatsana's mother reminded them.

"A good and happy year for you," Aunt Lavanny added with a big smile.

Vatsana didn't see how washing a picture and a statue was going to help her year all that much. But she wasn't going to say that to her mother or aunt. She wondered how much Ketsy believed in all that stuff.

It was raining, as usual. Vatsana didn't feel like going outside, so she went upstairs to her room. On an impulse, she took out the rectangle of weaving that her aunt Lavanny had brought her from Laos. She'd been keeping it in the bureau drawer where she put her socks and underwear.

She traced the slightly raised patterns of colored thread with her fingertips. The designs and the colors really were pretty. Maybe her father or Vyvone could make a frame for it and she could hang it on the wall. It looked different from her other pictures, but it might look nice somewhere in her room.

Vatsana was holding the weaving up to the wall, trying to decide where to put it, when Ketsy came into the room. Sometimes Vatsana still got irritated at having to share the room with Ketsy. But right now she was glad to see her.

"Can you hold this here for me?" she said in English. Ketsy was understanding more and more English these days.

"Okay," Ketsy said. She held the weaving against the wall above the bureau while Vatsana stepped back and looked at it.

"I think it looks good there," Vatsana said.

"I like it," Ketsy said in her slow English. "I'm happy you like too." She smiled at Vatsana and Vatsana smiled back. She was starting to like Ketsy more and more. She still didn't think the two of them were like sisters. But she was glad that she and Ketsy were cousins. It felt nice having a cousin in Portland.

At four-thirty, Becky and her mother arrived. Becky's mom was wearing an attractive light green skirt and a darker green blazer. Becky was wearing a gold and brown dress. They both left their shoes at the door, along with the row of shoes from Vatsana's family, even though Vatsana's mother said they didn't have to do that.

"Hi," Becky said. She smiled at Vatsana and Ketsy.

When everyone was sitting in the living room, Vatsana's mother asked Becky and her mom what they wanted to drink. She brought out a cup of tea for Becky's mom, a glass of pop for Becky, and a plate of little cakes for everyone. "I'm glad you can come to the New Year's celebration with us," Vatsana's mother said to Becky and her mom.

"I'm so glad you invited us," Becky's mom said.

"I'm sorry we won't have a better celebration today," Vatsana's mother said. "I think you will enjoy, but in Laos the celebration is much better."

"How would you celebrate the New Year if you were still in Laos?" Becky's mom asked.

"The New Year in Laos is a three-day holiday. On the first day we go to the temple. We bring perfumed water and we wash the statues of Buddha. That very lucky for the new year. Then we splash water on the monks and on each other." She smiled. "In Laos, April is much warmer than here in Portland. So we splash a lot of water and wash away anything bad we do in the old year. "At night we go back to the temple," Vatsana's mother continued. "The monks say prayers and then we follow them around the building three times. Everybody holds candles, so it's very beautiful."

"It does sound beautiful," Becky's mom said. Becky looked interested too, Vatsana saw.

"We visit our family and friends on the New Year and we eat special food and have a lot of fun. On the last day maybe a monk come to our house for a house-blessing ceremony. Then later we bring sand from the river to the temple. We make a hill with a banana plant on top and flowers and candles and sticks of incense all around. That brings us good luck for the coming year."

"That's a wonderful celebration," Becky's mom said. "I wish I could see it all sometime."

"Me too," Becky said.

It did sound nice, Vatsana agreed. She'd heard her mother talk about the New Year in Laos before, but of course she'd never seen it either. Her mother and father talked about going back to Laos for a visit if the new government would ever let them. Mostly Vatsana didn't feel very interested in doing that. But maybe if they went to Laos at the New Year, it would be fun. They could even go to Ban Keun, the village her mother told her stories about.

The New Year's celebration started at six o'clock but they wouldn't eat till seven or seven-thirty, so a lot of people wouldn't come until then. Vatsana's mother and aunt were going to help with the food, though, so her family needed to come on time.

The celebration was held at the community college this year. Vyvone went to school there, but Vatsana had never seen the college before. She looked around curiously at the concrete buildings and walkways, the posters and announcements tacked up on the walls. Maybe she would go to college here too when she was finished with high school. That all seemed pretty far away at the moment.

Vatsana's father had gotten their tickets in advance. At the table in the front of the cafeteria, he gave the tickets to the woman collecting them and wished her a good New Year.

Two girls who were standing near the ticket table pinned little ribbon bows on each of them and wished them a happy New Year. The girls were wearing Lao clothes—long embroidered skirts and silky tops with a satin sash across the chest and over one shoulder. They wore gold earrings and gold belts around their waists. Their hair was put up in a bun in the traditional Lao style.

"They look beautiful," Becky said.

"They do," Vatsana agreed. Still, she was glad that she wasn't wearing her Lao skirt. The *sin* was pretty, but she would feel funny wearing it around Becky and her mom. Anyway, almost all the people there were wearing regular American clothes.

Vatsana's father found a big table near the front where they would have a good view of the dancing. Up above the dance floor, crepe paper streamers were hanging from the ceiling. Vyvone laughed. "They really decorated up the old cafeteria. I hardly recognize it."

Vatsana was sitting between Becky and Ketsy. When Vatsana looked around her, she was glad to see another table where some Americans were sitting. Probably Becky and her mom were glad that they weren't the only Americans there, Vatsana thought. She didn't see David and his family anywhere though. Maybe they'd decided not to come, or maybe they were just coming a little later on.

More and more people kept coming in. Lots of people knew Vatsana's mother and father, so they came to their table to say hello to everyone and meet Aunt Lavanny and Ketsy, and Becky and her mom.

After a while most of the tables were filled up. Then the president of the Lao Association stood up in front of everyone and gave a speech, first in Lao, then in English. He welcomed them all there for the New Year's Celebration. *"Sok Dee Pee Mai,"* he said to them, which meant he wished them a lucky New Year.

When the president was finished, a couple of other people said a few words. One of them was Vatsana's father. "This is a good way to keep our Lao customs and celebrate together," he said to everybody. Vatsana thought he looked handsome in his best suit.

After Vatsana's father's talk, it was time to eat. They all lined up to get plates of food. "In Laos we would bring out big bowls of food and sit together and take what we want," Vatsana's mother explained to Becky's mom. "But here this way is easier."

The women standing behind the food line piled their plates high with food. There were

148

spring rolls, spicy fried chicken, fried rice, fried noodles which were crunchy and sweet, and Lao style salad. "It looks great," Becky said to Vatsana. "I just hope I can eat it all."

Vatsana grinned. "Me too." She was glad that Becky didn't act as if Lao food was too foreign or funny tasting.

After most people were finished eating, the dancing began. The first dance was a *lamvong*, the traditional Lao dance. The dancers made two big circles on the floor—men on the outside and women on the inside. The circles moved slowly around the room as the music was played. The dancers didn't touch each other as they danced, but they moved their hands in slow, graceful gestures. And everyone looked happy to be dancing at the Lao New Year celebration.

There was more dancing after that. The band played mostly Lao music but some American dances too. Vyvone danced with his girlfriend and Souk went outside the cafeteria to play with some other boys. Vatsana's mother and father danced a few times and Vatsana's father also danced with Vatsana's aunt Lavanny and with Becky's mom.

Ketsy had gone off with the boys and girls who were going to do the special Lao dances. Becky and Vatsana stood together along the side and watched the dancing. "You can do this kind of dancing, can't you?" Becky asked.

149

"A little," Vatsana said. "The way some of the women move their hands so gracefully. That's really hard to do." Vatsana laughed. "I guess my hands are too American to move like that."

Becky laughed too. "Remember when Ketsy tried to teach me. I didn't do too well either."

While they were watching the dancing, Vatsana saw David Stafford and his family arrive. They sat down at a table not too far from where Vatsana's family and Becky's mom were sitting. "Let's go say hello to them," Becky said. She smiled at Vatsana. "We can wish them a happy New Year."

David was glad to see them. He introduced them to his mother and father and his sister Barbara. She was in her first year of high school and seemed really nice. David's mother and father were friendly too and said they were glad to be at the New Year's celebration. "We would have come earlier," David's father said, "but we had a dinner we were already invited to."

"This is my mom," Becky said, as her mother came over to the table. After that Vatsana introduced David and his parents and sister to her mother and father and aunt Lavanny.

They all watched as a very little girl and a little boy, both of them in traditional Lao clothes, did a short dance together. They looked pretty cute, Vatsana thought. Then it was time for the dance performance that Ketsy was part of.

There were four girls and four boys in the dance. All of the girls were wearing long skirts with silver or gold embroidery, silk shirts, and bright red sashes over one shoulder. All the girls had flowers in their hair.

The boys wore black pants which ended just below their knees and black shirts. They carried a *khene,* drums, and bells to make music with.

The boys played music as they and the girls danced around the spirit jar, which was a big clay container with long straws coming from it. Both the girls and boys were smiling and having fun. One by one they went up to the jar and pretended to drink from the straws just as people in a Lao village would.

The girls danced especially gracefully. They had bare feet, and they balanced first on one foot then another, bowed and straightened. All the while they held their hands with their fingers bent into special positions and turned their hands slowly and gracefully.

"They're beautiful," Becky whispered.

Vatsana nodded. She hadn't realized how good a dancer Ketsy was or how beautiful she would look. Ketsy kept her balance perfectly and always looked graceful as she moved through the different positions of the dance.

When the dance was finished, everyone applauded. Ketsy came back and sat at their table, and everyone told her how good she had been. "You looked great," Vyvone said to her.

"You were beautiful up there," Vatsana's mother said.

Ketsy was smiling and looked really happy. Maybe the happiest she'd been since she came to the United States. Vatsana felt proud of Ketsy. "I think you were the best dancer," she said to her. Ketsy was a much better dancer than she'd ever be, but at the moment that didn't make her feel jealous.

Ketsy smiled at her and Becky. "Thank you," she said in English. "I like to dance at New Year."

The band started playing again, and people started dancing another *lamvong*. When the next dance was finished, a man who was a friend of Vatsana's father went to the microphone and called Vatsana's mother's name. She went up to the front and the man put a necklace of paper flowers on her. That meant the next dance was special for her, Vatsana explained to Becky. Mr. Viravong, Vatsana's father's friend, had bought that dance for Vatsana's father and mother to show that he loved and respected them.

Vatsana's mother and father were the first dancers in the *lamvong*, but other dancers quickly joined them. David's father and mother joined the circle, even though neither one of them knew how to do Lao dancing.

An older boy who had been in the dance performance with Ketsy asked her to dance. Then Vatsana's older brother Vyvone came over to where Vatsana, Becky, and David were sitting together. "Would you like to try the *lamvong*?" he asked Becky.

"Sure," Becky said enthusiastically. Vatsana knew Becky was always up for trying new things, and besides, Becky thought Vyvone was handsome.

"Do you want to try too?" David asked Vatsana. He looked a little embarrassed.

"Okay," Vatsana said. She felt shy again with David now. She hoped he really did want to dance with her. For sure, she'd never imagined that she would dance with David at the Lao New Year.

They joined the circle of dancers. Out of the corner of her eye, Vatsana watched David. He looked so funny trying to move his hands the way Lao people were doing that she forgot about her shyness and smiled at him. He grinned back at her. "This is a fun dance."

Becky and Vyvone were right in front of them. Becky couldn't do the dance right either but she looked as if she was enjoying herself. Becky was a good friend, Vatsana knew.

153

The *lamvong* wasn't anything like American dances. But Becky didn't seem to care. And Vatsana figured that David Stafford didn't either.

Neither of them were like Tom Connors. Tom thought anything different was bad. He was like the people in the Lao story her Aunt Lavanny had told. They thought the boy was bad just because his skin was dark. But the princess understood that the boy was fine the way he was, and she fell in love with him.

She really didn't care about Tom Connors, Vatsana thought. If he didn't like her just because her parents were from Laos, that was too bad.

She had been born in the United States and most of the time she felt as American as David and Becky. She didn't speak Lao or do Lao dancing as well as Ketsy did. She didn't feel like the graceful type either. But she was glad to be dancing the *lamvong* here tonight.

When the dance was over, most people went back to their seats. Vyvone went to sit with his girlfriend, and Vatsana, David, and Becky found their own table and sat together. A minute later, Ketsy came to join them.

"That was fun dancing," Becky said.

"It sure was," David agreed.

Vatsana smiled at both of them and at Ketsy too. She was happy to be here with

Becky, Ketsy, and David. She was glad all three of them were here with her to celebrate the Lao New Year.

Vatsana's mother had said that if Vatsana didn't know about Lao ideas, there would always be a missing part of her. But tonight Vatsana felt all here—the American part of her and the Lao part too. She didn't feel as though any pieces were missing.

"*Sok Dee Pee Mai,*" she said to Becky, Ketsy, and David—and to herself too. "Have a lucky New Year."

About the Author

Sara Gogol was born in Chicago but has lived in Portland, Oregon, long enough that she almost feels like a native. She used to teach English as a Second Language to students from many different countries, including refugees from Southeast Asia. Currently she teaches English composition and literature at a community college. She writes fiction and nonfiction for children and adults. In her free time, she enjoys gardening and playing with her two dogs, Katy and Yarrow.